"Do you realise you have me at a complete disadvantage?" Salvatore observed slowly. **"You seem to know exactly who I am, while I have no idea what your name is."**

Lina took another sip before replying and the sweet-sharp taste of the lemons was icy against her lips. "It's Nicolina Vitale," she said. "But my friends call me Lina."

There was a heartbeat of a pause. "And what would you like me to call you?"

His question hung on the air—as fragile as a bubble. An innocent question that suddenly didn't feel innocent at all because the smokiness in his eyes was making her want to tremble, despite the heat of the day. Lina was a stranger to flirting, mainly because she'd never met anyone she'd wanted to flirt with, but suddenly she was finding it easy. As easy as the smile she slanted him, as if she mixed with handsome billionaires every day of the week.

"You can call me Lina," she said huskily.

Sharon Kendrick once won a national writing competition by describing her ideal date: being flown to an exotic island by a gorgeous and powerful man. Little did she realize that she'd just wandered into her dream job! Today she writes for Harlequin, and her books feature often stubborn but always *to-die-for* heroes and the women who bring them to their knees. She believes that the best books are those you never want to end. Just like life...

Books by Sharon Kendrick

Harlequin Presents

The Italian's Christmas Housekeeper

Conveniently Wed!

Bound to the Sicilian's Bed
The Greek's Bought Bride
His Contract Christmas Bride

One Night With Consequences

The Pregnant Kavakos Bride
The Italian's Christmas Secret
Crowned for the Sheikh's Baby

Secret Heirs of Billionaires

The Sheikh's Secret Baby

The Legendary Argentinian Billionaires

Bought Bride for the Argentinian
The Argentinian's Baby of Scandal

Visit the Author Profile page
at Harlequin.com for more titles.

Sharon Kendrick

—

CINDERELLA IN THE SICILIAN'S WORLD

HARLEQUIN
PRESENTS

HARLEQUIN®
PRESENTS®

PLEASE RECYCLE
THIS PRODUCT IS RECYCLABLE

Recycling programs
for this product may
not exist in your area.

ISBN-13: 978-1-335-14834-6

Cinderella in the Sicilian's World

Copyright © 2020 by Sharon Kendrick

This edition published by arrangement with Harlequin Books S.A.

For questions and comments about the quality of this book, please contact us at CustomerService@Harlequin.com.

Harlequin Enterprises ULC
22 Adelaide St. West, 40th Floor
Toronto, Ontario M5H 4E3, Canada
www.Harlequin.com

Printed in U.S.A.

CINDERELLA IN THE
SICILIAN'S WORLD

For my father, Donald Llewelyn Wirdnam—one of life's truly contented people, whose favorite toast will never be forgotten (and neither will he).

"Here's to my wife's husband!"

PROLOGUE

SALVATORE DI LUCA stared out at the bright blue Sicilian sea and felt his heart twist with something he had spent years trying to avoid. With pain. With regret. And with a bitter awareness that he had never really loved this beautiful island as much as he should have done. But how could he love it when it was bound up with so many bitter memories of the past? A past he had tried many times to escape, sometimes with more success than others.

Because wherever he went, he always took the past with him.

On this island he had possessed nothing and had known hunger. Real hunger. His clothes had been ragged and—when he hadn't been running through the streets barefoot—his shoes second-hand. It had been a long time since he'd known hunger like that. A long time since he'd wanted for anything. These days he had everything which had once been his heart's desire. There were properties around the world in addition to his San Franciscan home—a vineyard in Tuscany, a castle in Spain, and, up until very recently, a *pied-à-terre* in Paris. He had planes and cars and an Icelandic river in which to fish, whenever the whim took him. His property business had long been in the ascendancy and these days he channelled his profits into his charitable foundation, which reached out to children the world over. Dispossessed children. Children who had never been loved. Children just like him.

And there were women. Plenty of those. Beautiful, sophisticated, elegant women. He dated lawyers and bankers. Heiresses and scientists. He was highly sought after as a partner—his skill as a lover, his quick mind and vast personal wealth made sure of that. The only thing he couldn't provide was love, because that had been removed from his heart a long time ago and that was what inevitably proved to be the death-knell on any relationship, for women craved love even when they had been warned it was never going to be on the cards.

In theory, he should have been perfectly content. Didn't his friends—and his enemies—think he'd forged for himself the perfect life? And didn't he allow them to carry on believing that? But occasionally he became aware of an aching emptiness deep at the very core of him, rumbling away in the background, like an incipient thunderstorm on the dark horizon. Sometimes he didn't think that ache would ever leave him and sometimes he told himself it was better that way.

Because the memories which provoked that pain made him certain of what he did want, but equally important—what he didn't. And if that knowledge had turned him into someone who was perceived as cold and unfeeling, then so be it. Let people think what they wanted.

It was time to embrace his freedom and drink a toast to it.

Turning away from the blinding glare of the ocean, Salvatore lifted his hand, and summoned over the waiter who had been hovering within his eyeline for the last half-hour.

The funeral was over and the inevitable introspection which followed such an event was also over. It was time to move on.

CHAPTER ONE

'WHAT THE *HELL* do you think you're doing, Nicolina?'

The words sounded sharp. Sharp as the tip of a needle or the sting of a bee. Lina's throat tightened as she pulled the thin cotton blouse over her head and turned to meet the accusing gaze of the woman who had just entered her bedroom. Not for the first time, she wished her mother would knock before she came barging in, but she guessed that would be like wishing for the stars.

'I thought I'd go for a drive,' she said, winding a scrunchie around her thick hair, even though trying to get her black curls to obey her was a daily battle.

'Dressed like *that*?'

The word was delivered viciously and Lina wondered what had caused this reaction, because no way could her outfit have offended her mother's overdeveloped sense of decency. 'Like what?' she questioned, genuinely confused.

Her mother's look of contempt was moving from the modest shirt, down to the perfectly decent pair of handmade denim culottes, which Lina had run up on her old sewing machine only last week, from some leftover fabric she'd managed to find lying around the workshop. According to the pages of one of the online fashion journals, which she devoured whenever she got the chance, they could have done with being at least five inches shorter, but what would have been the point in showing too much flesh? Why make unnecessary waves and have to listen to a constant background noise of criticism, when she spent most of her time trying to block it out?

'You are supposed to be in mourning!'

Lina felt the urge to protest that the elderly man who had recently died was someone she'd never even met and whose funeral she had only attended because that was what people did in this tiny Sicilian village where she'd lived all her life. But she resisted the desire to say so because she didn't want a row. Not when she was feeling so flat and so vulnerable, for reasons she didn't dare analyse.

'The funeral is over, Mama,' she said quietly. 'And even the chief mourner has left.' For hadn't Salvatore di Luca—the billionaire godson of the recently deceased—purred away in his car that very morning, leaving Lina staring glumly as the shiny limousine retreated down the mountainside, knowing she would never see him again? And wondering why that should bother her so much.

You know why. Because whenever he looked at you he made you feel alive. Because that was his skill. His special ability. To make women melt whenever he flicked that hooded blue gaze over them.

His occasional visits to her village had been something to look forward to. Like Christmas, or birthdays. Something shining bright in the future, which she would never see again. And somehow that left her feeling like a balloon which had just been popped.

'Salvatore di Luca!' Her mother's voice broke into her thoughts as she spat out his name, with even more contempt than she had displayed towards Lina's outfit. 'In the old days he would have stayed for at least a week to pay his respects to the community. But I suppose his fame and fortune are more important than the Sicilian roots he has turned his back on in favour of his new and fancy *American* life!'

Lina didn't agree with her mother's condemnation but there was little point in arguing. Because her mother was always right, wasn't she? Early widowhood had given her the moral high ground, as well as an increasing bitterness towards the world in general as the years passed by. And with that bitterness had come a highly sophisticated ability to create a feeling of guilt in her only child. To make her feel as if she were somehow responsible for her mother's woes. And wasn't that state of affairs becoming increasingly intolerable? Picking up her helmet, Lina made a passable attempt at a smile though she met no answering smile in response. 'There's been a lot going on, Mama. I just…need a break.'

'Oh, that I were twenty-eight years old again! When I was your age I never used to complain about tiredness. I was too busy running this business almost single-handed. You are too young to be *taking a break*. When I was your age I never stopped,' her mother mocked. 'And there's work for you here.'

Of course there was. There was always work for her here. Lina toiled from dawn to dusk in the family's small dressmaking business, running up cheap skirts and dresses which would later be sold on one of the island's many markets, with barely a word of thanks from the woman who had birthed her. But she didn't really expect any, if the truth be known. Obedience had been drummed into her for as long as she could remember—even before her father had died so young, leaving her to bear the full brunt of her mother's ire. And Lina had accepted what fate had bequeathed her because that was what village girls like her had always done. They worked hard, they obeyed their parents and behaved respectably and one day they married and produced a family of their own—and so the whole cycle was repeated.

But Lina had never married. She'd not even come close—and not because there hadn't been the opportunity. She'd caused outrage and consternation in the village by rejecting the couple of suitors who had called for her, with their wilting bunches of flowers and sly eyes, which had strayed lecherously to the over-abundant thrust of her breasts. She had decided she would prefer to be on her own than to sacrifice herself to the unimaginable prospect of sharing a bed with either of those two men. It was a black mark against her of course. For an only child, a failure to produce a clutch of grandchildren would not easily be forgiven. And although Lina didn't regret either of those two decisions, it sometimes left her with the feeling that she had somehow burnt her boats. That she would remain here for the rest of her days and that this was to be her future.

As her mother slammed her way out of the bedroom, Lina was aware that nothing had really changed in her life since yesterday's funeral, yet she was aware that something had changed inside *her*. It had been a busy time—especially for the womenfolk, who had been preparing all the food which had been consumed by the mourners. They had buried Paolo Cardinelli with all the honour and ceremony with which Sicily traditionally regarded the deceased. But now it was over and life went on and Lina had been struck by the realisation that time was stretching out in front of her like an uninspiring road. Suddenly she felt trapped by the towering walls of oppression and expectation and her mother's endless demands.

And she needed to escape.

She didn't really have a plan. Her best friend lived in a neighbouring mountain village and often they would meet for a coffee. But their friendship had taken a hit since Rosa's recent marriage and travelling solo to one of the fancier seaside resorts at the foot of the mountain wouldn't usually have been on Lina's agenda. Yet today she felt like breaking a few of her own self-imposed rules. Scrabbling at the back of the wardrobe to locate some of the money she'd stashed away from her ridiculously small wages, she found herself itching for a different experience. For something *new*.

Pausing only to stuff her swimsuit in the back of her rucksack, she wheeled out her little scooter and accelerated away from the village, the dust from the dry streets billowing up in clouds around her. Past the last straggle of houses on the edge of the village she negotiated the winding bends, and a sudden unexpected sense of freedom lifted her spirits as she sped downwards towards the coast. She could smell the sea before she saw it—a wide ribbon of cobalt glittering brightly in the afternoon sunshine and it smelt delicious.

Breathing in the salty air, she drove towards

a beach famous for its natural beauty. It was the kind of place where people spent vast amounts of money to lie beneath fringed umbrellas and have iced drinks brought to them on trays. The kind of place she would usually have dismissed as being too grand and too fancy for someone like her. But today? Her heart pumped as she parked her bike close to the seafront bar. Today she felt different. She felt almost *fatalistic.*

Lina walked towards the open-air bar, acutely aware of how much she stood out from the rich tourists with their glitzy beach outfits and gold jewellery, but since she would never see any of these people again—did it really matter? She would perch on one of those tall bar stools and enjoy an icy sharp *granita* and afterwards drive off to her favourite secluded cove and have a swim. Pulling off her helmet and tucking it beneath her arm, she was shaking out her long hair as she picked her way along the sand-covered decking towards the beach bar.

And that was when she saw him.

Her knees went weak and something powerful unfurled low in her belly as she stared at the man who was sitting in the shade of the awning, effortlessly dominating the space around him, and Lina could feel the sudden racing of her heart as her gaze drank him in. Because it was him.

Him.

What were the chances?

Salvatore di Luca was perched on one of the tall bar stools, staring at his cell phone, seemingly oblivious to the fact that he was attracting the gaze of every person in the place, though surely he must have been used to it by now. Hadn't the eyes of every villager been fixed on him from the moment he'd stepped from his chauffeur-driven car onto Caltarina's dusty main street for his godfather's funeral? Hadn't women—of every age—surreptitiously patted their hair and pulled their shoulders back, as if unconsciously longing for him to gaze with admiration on their breasts?

And hadn't Lina been one of them? Struck dumb by his potent presence. By his thick dark hair and bright blue eyes.

He was still wearing the required black funeral attire—an exquisitely cut suit, as her professional eye had noted earlier, which emphasised the innate strength rippling through his muscular frame. His only concession to the powerful heat had been to remove his jacket and tie and undo the top two buttons of his shirt, but he still stood out from the carelessly dressed holidaymakers like a forbidding dark cloud which had moved dangerously close to the glare of the sun.

Lina hesitated as she glanced down at the grains of sand which were clinging to her well-worn trainers, uncertain whether to introduce herself and say something, because surely that would be the right thing to do in the circumstances. To tell him she was very sorry about his godfather. Though what if he just looked through her blankly? He certainly wouldn't have noticed her back in Caltarina—he had been too busy dealing with the attentions of the village elders who had surrounded him from the moment he'd arrived. And since he didn't come from around here, he didn't really know anyone by name. Yes, she had sometimes seen him from a distance when he had paid one of his unannounced visits, but she'd never actually spoken to him. Like her, most people in the village had simply gazed at him in wonder, as you might gaze on some bright star if it had tumbled down from the night sky.

Should she go up and offer him her condolences, or leave the poor man in peace? She almost smiled at the wildly inaccurate track of her thoughts because *poor* was the last word you'd ever use to describe a man like Salvatore di Luca. Even living in a village which sometimes felt like the land time had forgotten, none of Caltarina's inhabitants could have failed to be aware of the fortune and wealth of the powerful tycoon.

She decided it was best to slip away unnoticed, but he chose just that moment to slide the cell phone into his jacket and to lift his head. His eyes narrowed and then refocussed and he appeared to be staring. At *her*. Lina blinked, half tempted to turn around to see if there was someone else he might have recognised standing behind her. Someone as rich and as beautiful as him. But no, his gaze was definitely on her. It was piercing through her like a bright sword and Lina felt momentarily disconcerted by his arresting beauty. Because…those eyes! Those incredible blue eyes, which were rumoured to be a throwback to the days when Greek warriors had conquered the jewelled island of Sicily. Hadn't she overheard women whispering about their astonishing hue, not long after the coffin had been lowered deep into the hard, unforgiving soil? Talking about a man so avidly at such a time was perhaps a little disrespectful, but in a way Lina couldn't blame them. Because wasn't Salvatore di Luca the embodiment of everything it meant to be virile and masculine, and who wouldn't be tempted to comment on something like that?

And now…

She blinked.

Now he was beckoning her over with an imperious curl of his finger as if he wanted her to join him and Lina froze with indecision and hope.

Surely there had to be some sort of mistake. Maybe he'd got her muddled up with someone else. Maybe he didn't mean her at all. And yet she found herself praying he did. That she could go over there and join him and for one afternoon forget she was Lina Vitale, the poor dressmaker who lived in a forgotten mountain village. The woman who seemed to observe life from a distance as it swiftly passed her by...

Salvatore narrowed his eyes as he stared at the dark-haired beauty with the windswept hair, pleased to have a diversion from the disturbing cycle of his thoughts. He recognised her, of course. Even though she'd been one of a multitude of women wearing black, she had the kind of curves which nature had designed to imprint onto a man's memory, as well as the softest pair of lips he had ever seen, and naturally a man would register those facts, almost as a matter of course.

He wondered if she had followed him here. It happened. In fact, it happened a lot. He was pursued frequently and without shame, and while some men might have chosen to capitalise on the potential for such easy seduction, Salvatore wasn't one of them. Given a preference, he preferred to be the hunter— though these days, most women seemed oblivious to that simple fact.

The Sicilian woman who stood on the other side of the bar was worlds away from the type of woman he usually dated, yet, despite this, Salvatore's gaze flickered over her with interest. She certainly looked out of place in this chic bar with her commonplace outfit and a dusty motorbike helmet, which was tucked beneath her arm. But the dark curls which bounced down her back were lustrous and glossy and her denim culottes emphasised the undulating swell of her generous hips. And her breasts were luscious, their firm swell emphasising her innate femininity.

He felt an unmistakable prickle of interest. Hers was one of those old-fashioned figures he rarely encountered in his busy transatlantic life, or at home in San Francisco, where he was surrounded by wafer-thin socialites, whose main aim in life seemed to be to maintain an abnormally low body weight. He wondered whether to offer to buy her a drink. Surely it would be bad manners to ignore her—particularly as she had done him the courtesy of paying her respects to his godfather. Lifting his finger, he beckoned her over and, after a moment of hesitation he wasn't expecting, she walked slowly towards him, a faint flush of colour highlighting her sculpted cheekbones as he rose to his feet to greet her.

'Signor di Luca,' she said, when at last she reached him, her obvious nerves making her words trip over themselves. 'I didn't mean to disturb you. I... I saw you at your godfather's funeral.'

He had to bend his head to hear her properly, for her voice was soft and melodic and her faltering words rang with such genuine condolence that Salvatore felt a wave of unexpected emotion washing over him. It wasn't the first time this had happened since he'd learned that his godfather had died, but it was hard for him to get his head around, because he was a man who didn't *do* emotion. He was someone who prided himself on his detachment and had told himself repeatedly that the old man had been given a happy release from his earthly bonds.

For although he owed a deep sense of gratitude to the man whose generosity had allowed him to spread his wings and leave his native land, he had never loved him. He had never loved anyone since his mother's callous and brutal rejection.

So why had his eyes prickled with tears and his heart contracted with pain when he had been taken to view the cold and silent body of his godfather? Why had he felt as if something had ended without him quite knowing what it was?

'And I'm very sorry for your loss,' the curvy brunette was saying, biting her voluptuous bottom lip rather nervously.

'*Grazie.* He is at peace now after a long illness, and for that I give thanks.' Salvatore watched as she chewed her bottom lip again and as he found himself increasingly fixated on that dark, rosy cushion an idea occurred to him, which he was finding impossible to shift. 'You are meeting someone?' he probed softly.

She shook her head. 'No. No, I'm all alone. I came on a whim,' she answered and then shrugged rather apologetically, as if aware of having given more information than he'd asked for.

'Then you will join me for a drink?' he questioned, inclining his head towards the vacant stool next to him. 'Or perhaps you disapprove of the fact that I am sitting in the sunshine, listening to the sound of the sea at such a time, when my godfather was buried only yesterday and now lies deep beneath the soil?'

Again, she shook her head and her thick black curls shimmered in the light sea breeze. 'I make no such judgment,' she said, placing her helmet on the bar and wriggling onto the bar stool he was holding out for her. 'In the village you must have noticed people chattering even while they carried the coffin towards the cemetery. It is always like that. Life goes on,' she continued, with a quiet rush of confidence. 'Such is the way of the world.'

She sounded both old and wise as she spoke, as if she were repeating the words of her elders, and Salvatore's eyes narrowed as he tried to guess her age because that was a safer bet than focussing on her delicious bottom. Late-twenties, he thought. Possibly more.

'In many ways, my godfather's death was a blessed release,' he said, staring into dark-lashed eyes which were the colour of the old and expensive bourbon he'd first encountered when he'd arrived in America, so young and so very angry. And something in those eyes made him confide in her about the old man's final years. 'You are aware that he lay in a coma this past decade?' he questioned. 'Not seeing, not speaking and possibly not hearing anything which went on around him?'

She nodded. 'Yes, I do. One of my friends was one of the many carers you employed to look after him, Signor di Luca. We thought it was wonderful you didn't move him out of the village into some big institution in the city. Particularly as you are a stranger to these parts. And of course, everyone knows that you visited regularly, which couldn't have been easy for a man as busy as you must be.' She hesitated. 'You are very kind.'

Salvatore tensed, briefly startled by her words because this wasn't a character assessment he was used to. Unsolicited praise wasn't something which came his way very often, unless from women cooing over his prowess in bed. Yes, he was often applauded for his business acumen and ability to be ahead of the curve. And, yes, he was a significant philanthropist. But to be commended for his personal kindness? That really was a one-off. As he looked at her sweet face he felt the stir of something unrecognisable deep in his heart. Something which did not sit easily with him. Was it the realisation that, suddenly, he really *was* all alone in the world? Even though his godfather had not been sentient for over ten years, he was his last and only link with his past.

Salvatore shook his head, as if he could dislodge the dark thoughts which were stubbornly refusing to shift. He needed a distraction, he decided, and here was one sitting next to him in the shape of this local beauty. But would it be wise to pursue such a diversion? He examined his motives for wanting her to stay. He didn't want to seduce her. Hell, no. Not only was she most definitely not his type, she probably had a fistful of vengeful brothers and uncles who would demand he married her if he went within touching distance!

But the thought of spending a couple of uncomplicated hours in her company and letting her naïve chatter wash over him was suddenly appealing. Besides, wasn't there something a little *careworn* about her features? As if she had been carrying the weight of the world on her shoulders. A moment of unfamiliar compassion spiralled up inside him as he came to a rapid conclusion.

'Do you have to rush away?'

Lina narrowed her eyes, wondering if she'd heard him correctly but also wondering what had caused that intense look of pain to have crossed his face. Was he thinking about his godfather, or had it been something else? She reflected how strange life could be sometimes. When here was a man who appeared to have everything, yet for a moment back then his expression had seemed almost...*haunted*.

He was waiting for an answer to his question and she knew exactly what she should say. Thank him politely but decline. Walk away from the bar and the faint sense of edginess he exuded, while reminding herself that she and this man had nothing in common. Some bone-deep instinct warned her he could be dangerous—and who in their right mind would willingly embrace danger? But vying with that certainty was something stronger. Something which was telling her to do the very opposite. Hadn't she driven away from the village today precisely *because* she wanted to experience something different—and wasn't this her opportunity to do just that?

Up this close, his proximity was making her body react in a way which was shocking yet delicious. Her nipples had begun to tighten beneath her handmade blouse—and now a low curl of heat was pulsing somewhere deep inside her and setting her blood on fire. Was this what it was all about? she wondered as she felt her lips grow dry. Was this what all her friends chattered about—a desire which had always eluded her up until now?

'No, I don't have to rush away.'

'Then will you have a glass of wine with me?' A

flicker of humour danced in the azure depths of his eyes. 'Are you old enough to drink?'

He was flattering her, she knew that. But Lina shook her head. She didn't want wine. She wanted as clear a head as possible. 'No, thank you,' she said. 'It's much too hot. I'd like a *granita*, please.'

'A *granita*,' he repeated thoughtfully. 'I haven't had one of those in years.'

He ordered two and the granitas were delivered in chunky little glasses clouded with condensation and it wasn't until after they had drunk for a moment, in silence, that the Sicilian tycoon turned to her again.

'Do you realise you have me at a complete disadvantage?' he observed slowly. 'You seem to know exactly who I am, while I have no idea what your name is.'

She took another sip before replying and the sweet-sharp taste of the lemons was icy against her lips. And wasn't it bizarre that her senses suddenly seemed *raw*, so that the *granita* tasted better than any *granita* she'd ever had, and the glittering sea had never appeared bluer than it did right now?

'It's Nicolina Vitale,' she said. 'But my friends call me Lina.'

There was a heartbeat of a pause. 'And what would you like me to call you?'

His question hung on the air—as fragile as a bubble. An innocent question which suddenly didn't feel innocent at all because the smokiness in his eyes was making her want to tremble, despite the heat of the day. Lina was a stranger to flirting, mainly because she'd never met anyone she'd wanted to flirt with, but suddenly she was finding it easy. As easy as the smile she slanted him, as if she mixed with handsome billionaires every day of the week.

'You can call me Lina,' she said huskily.

His blue eyes hardened with something she didn't recognise, but it was gone so quickly that she didn't have time to analyse it.

'So are you going to stay here for a while, Lina Vitale?' he was enquiring softly. 'Are you going to throw caution to the wind and have lunch with me?'

Lina was aware of a sudden rush of colour to her cheeks as briefly she wondered what her friend Rosa would say if she could see her now. She wouldn't be teasing her about being a cold fish, would she? And those two spurned suitors would have been forced to retract their cruel comments about her being uptight and frigid.

'Why not?' she said shyly, and gave him a breathless smile.

CHAPTER TWO

THE AFTERNOON SUN was low in the sky and people were beginning to make their way back to the sun-beds now that the fierce heat of midday had subsided. Against the ocean's glitter, Lina could see women on loungers reapplying suncream and thought how cool and composed they all looked.

Unlike her. It was hot down here on the sand and her body was reacting to it in a way which wasn't particularly attractive. Sweat was beading her fore-head beneath her thick curls and her clothes were sticking to her skin. She shifted a little in her seat, still unable to believe she was having lunch with a world-famous tycoon.

She wondered if she'd outstayed her welcome. Probably. Though since she had no experience of this kind of affair, it was impossible to know. But surely someone like Salvatore di Luca must have grown bored with the conversational limitations of a village girl by now. Maybe it was time she gave him an exit route.

Pushing her plate away, she glanced up into his arresting face and, once again, her heart gave a powerful punch of pleasure. 'I guess it's time I was going.'

'You don't say that with any degree of conviction,' he observed, an unfathomable expression darkening his ruggedly handsome face. 'And you've barely touched your lunch.'

This much was true. Lina felt a rush of guilt as she stared at her plate. She was fond of her food and had been brought up never to waste anything and certainly not a meal as expensive as this. But she'd barely been able to swallow a morsel. The food had tasted like sawdust and her throat had felt tight with a tension she couldn't seem to shift. Because beneath the fierce light of Salvatore's potent charisma, she could feel her senses unfurling. As if the cautious and inexperienced Lina Vitale was blossoming into someone she didn't recognise, dazzled by the attentions of a man who was little more than a handsome stranger.

He had commandeered a shaded table which sat on the edge of the sea, where, after a little persuasion, she had removed her socks and trainers so that her bare toes could wriggle luxuriously in the sand. Then she'd sat back in her chair watching the crystal blue waters lapping against the crushed silver shore, as armies of waiters rushed over to serve them. It was the most luxurious thing which had happened in her twenty-eight years and Lina found herself savouring every moment. Terrified of doing the wrong thing, she'd watched Salvatore closely throughout the meal to make sure she didn't let herself down. But he had surprised her. He hadn't behaved remotely how she thought a billionaire *would* behave. He hadn't ordered lobster or scallops or any of the fancier items which adorned the menu. Instead, he had rolled up the sleeves of his white silk shirt and devoured his meal as hungrily as any labourer and Lina had been surprised at his very traditional choice of tomato sauce, fried aubergine and ricotta cheese.

'I didn't notice it on the menu,' she said.

'That's because it isn't. But they always make it for me when I come here.'

'Was it something your mother used to cook?' she guessed.

As far as she was aware, it was the only awkward part of the meal for his face suddenly grew cold. Cold as the ice bobbing around in her glass of sparkling water. Suddenly his voice sounded like stone. 'No,' he clipped out. 'My mother wasn't into *cooking*.'

She found herself wishing she could take the words back and attempted to lighten the mood by asking other questions, more questions about his life, and he filled in some of the gaps which village gossip had been unable to provide. He told her that he'd been a humble waiter in America when he had overheard his boss complaining how difficult it was to transfer money internationally. At the time, Salvatore had been doing a course on digital technology at night school and this one remark had inspired him to invent an amazingly simple phone app which solved just that problem. He'd made a fortune in the process.

'Just like that?' Lina asked, wide-eyed.

'Just like that,' he agreed.

'And then what did you do?'

He then went on to explain that he had diversified, buying up property and department stores and a small airplane company which chartered rich passengers between the different Caribbean islands. And when he'd made more money than any man could spend in a hundred lifetimes, he poured his funds into a charitable foundation for children, set up in his name.

But he seemed more interested in talking about *her*, though Lina couldn't quite shake off the feeling that he was regarding her with the interest one might display towards an unusual exhibit at the zoo. Maybe he saw her as some kind of relic as she chattered away about the family dressmaking business. Like some sort of curiosity.

She remembered his stand-out incredulous question.

'So you've never even been abroad?'

'I almost did once,' she replied, a little defensively. 'Last year, I was supposed to go to Florida for my cousin's wedding and I was going to spend a little time working out there, but...'

'But?' he probed.

'My mother got ill and said she'd rather I didn't go, so I didn't.'

'Let me guess—she got better straight away?'

'She did, yes. How did you know that?'

He had given a bitter laugh. 'Human nature. Otherwise known as manipulation. You don't need to be a genius to work it out.'

But now the empty coffee cups and scatter of *amaretti* crumbs on the table indicated that the meal was well and truly over and Lina was aware that she really ought to make a move.

'I'd better go,' she said again.

'You sound as if you don't want to go anywhere,' he observed, lifting his fingers in a careless gesture, which instantly had a waiter scurrying towards them with the bill. 'Is there something special you need to be back for?'

Lina couldn't help the feeling of dread which fluttered inside her stomach as she reached beneath the table to retrieve her trainers and wondered what he'd say if he knew what she was really going home to. Not the pared-down and slightly amusing version of village life with which she'd regaled him, but her mother's sour face and incessant demands. Cheap denim and cotton stacked into high piles, waiting for her to turn them into skirts and shirts and knock-off designer dresses. The endless hours alone with her whirring sewing machine and then those long and desperately lonely evenings which followed—the silence broken only by the constant chiming of the church bells. Suddenly it all seemed so empty—and more than a little bit sad. Was that what made her look into his eyes with a sudden rush of resolve, which was accompanied by an unfamiliar sense of defiance?

'Not really, no,' she said. 'I'll have to get back in time for dinner, of course.'

'Of course.' There was the merest flicker of a pause as he deposited a wad of notes on top of the bill and his blue eyes were shuttered when he glanced up at her again. He slid his wallet back into his jacket pocket. 'Well, then. What would you have been doing this afternoon if you hadn't bumped into me?'

Lina thought about it. She would have driven to her favourite hidden cove, hoping that nobody else would be there. And, after swimming until she was cool and pleasantly tired, she would be attempting to brush the stubborn sand from her body and perform-ing a few clumsy acrobatics as she tried to modestly remove her swimsuit from behind a towel. 'I was planning on going swimming,' she said.

He looked across at the rows of loungers which were laid in neat lines. 'Swimming?' he repeated. 'You mean here?'

Lina followed his gaze, noting that the occupants of the loungers wore bikinis which were little more than a series of flimsy triangles, which someone as curvy as her would never be able to get away with. She thought about the swimsuit she'd stuffed at the bottom of her rucksack. Imagine the reaction if she took to this exclusive beach wearing *that*! She'd probably be frogmarched straight off for committing a crime against fashion!

'No, not here,' she said quickly. 'This beach is private. Only guests of the hotel are allowed to use it.'

'Oh, don't worry about that,' he said, with the cool confidence of a man for whom no door was ever closed. 'Nobody's going to stop you from swimming.'

Not while you're with me, went the unspoken subtext but Lina still shook her head. 'No, honestly,' she said quickly, unable to keep the sudden panic from her voice. 'Forget I ever said it. I don't... I don't really want to swim here, if it's all the same with you.'

He gave her a considered look. 'Well, what about a swim at my villa, if you don't want an audience?'

Lina's throat thickened with an emotion she didn't recognise. Just as she didn't recognise the sudden hopeful squeak of her voice. 'You mean you're staying here? In Sicily?'

He shrugged. 'Only tonight. My plane will take me back to San Francisco tomorrow.'

'I don't want to put you to any trouble.'

'It's no trouble. My car is outside.'

'So is my scooter.'

'So why don't I get my chauffeur to ride your bike for you, and I can drive you to my villa myself? You can have a swim and leave when you like.'

'Won't your chauffeur mind driving my scooter?'

'He isn't paid to *mind*,' he drawled arrogantly. 'He's paid very handsomely to do exactly what I tell him to do.'

Salvatore watched as she worried her bottom lip again, a gesture which left her mouth looking so unbelievably kissable that he wondered if it was done for precisely that effect. He was used to instant acquiescence—especially from women—but Lina Vitale kept him waiting for an answer and the novelty of that was more than a little exciting.

'Okay,' she said eventually, pushing a thick handful of hair back from her face. 'Why not?'

Why not? Salvatore frowned. She obviously didn't realise that he wasn't usually given to handing out invitations to waifs and strays and that a little gratitude might have been welcome. He pushed back his chair. He couldn't work her out. Not only that—but he still hadn't quite worked out his own motives for inviting her. Was he intending to seduce her? To peel off those over-long denim shorts and the almost puritanical cotton shirt to see what voluptuous delights lay beneath?

His mouth hardened. No. He had never been into one-night stands and even if he were he certainly wouldn't choose a woman from a tiny mountain village who would probably read too much into it. He was being kind, that was all. Hadn't she praised him for such kindness earlier?

So stop being such a cynical bastard and make the poor woman's day.

'Come on, then. Let's go,' he said abruptly, rising to his feet and causing a woman on a nearby table to completely miss her mouth as she prepared to take a drink of wine.

As Lina had suspected, Salvatore's chauffeur looked distinctly unimpressed at being presented with her helmet and told to drive her scooter. But he didn't protest. His bulky body dwarfed the small fifty cc machine, but by then Salvatore was opening the passenger door of the limousine and Lina was climbing inside. And, oh, it was gorgeous. It smelt of leather and wealth, and the powerful engine made less noise than her hairdryer as Salvatore drove along familiar roads before turning onto a hidden track on the opposite side of the mountain.

And this, Lina quickly realised, was a completely different world from the one she usually inhabited. A quietly wealthy part of the island, where rich tourists parted with huge amounts of money in order to be able to live the Sicilian dream—or rather, their version of that dream. But it was difficult to concentrate on the scenic beauty of these new surroundings. Difficult to look anywhere other than at the powerful thrust of Salvatore's thighs.

'Comfortable?' he questioned obliquely.

'Very,' she lied.

The shades he had donned made him seem even more sexy and inaccessible than before. *Because he is inaccessible,* she reminded herself fiercely. *He's a hunky billionaire who's got a whole different life on the other side of the world.* But none of those thoughts seemed to have any effect on her escalating excitement. It didn't stop her breasts from hardening, or lessen the imperceptible tension which seemed to be building between them within the confined space of the car. Soon, it had reached such a pitch that Lina felt as if she'd forgotten how to breathe normally, and as a pair of ornate iron gates swung silently open she reached into her rucksack and surreptitiously turned off her phone, determined that nobody was going to disturb this day, least of all her mother. Because this was a one-off. She knew that. She wasn't going to entertain any unrealistic expectations or try to second-guess what was about to happen, she was simply going to enjoy every second of it.

'Madonna mia!' she breathed, unguarded pleasure slipping from her lips as the gates closed behind them. 'Is this for real?'

A faint smile touched the edges of his lips. 'Do you like it?'

'Yes,' she breathed. 'Yes, I like it.' Alighting from the car, she stood in the courtyard and stared up at an imposing house, surrounded by tall palm trees which soared up into the bright blueness of the sky. Dotted around the place were antique terracotta pots containing bright flowers and in the distance she could see the dark glitter of a swimming pool.

A housekeeper appeared from within the shadowed entrance of the house—a sharp-eyed woman wearing black who failed to return her nervous smile of greeting. But Lina heaved a silent sigh of relief because at least she didn't recognise the woman as being from Caltarina. How difficult would that have been?

'Carla, could you please arrange to have coffee sent down to the pool?' Salvatore's voice was smooth and entitled, before turning to Lina. 'Come with me and I'll show you where you can change.'

Lina followed him through the grounds, telling herself she should be enjoying every aspect of this lovely garden, but it wasn't flowers or shrubs she wanted to look at, and it wasn't the exotic cacti or carefully positioned statues which were dominating her attention. She couldn't seem to tear her eyes away from Salvatore's broad shoulders where the thick black waves of his hair were curving decadently over his collar and making her wonder what it would be like to trickle her fingers through them. She stared at the fluid thrust of his hips as he walked along the path with a confident stealth which radiated power and strength.

At last they came to a vast infinity pool—its water as dark as sapphires—with panoramic views over the green and golden countryside. But even that knockout view didn't have any impact on her sudden overwhelming sense of self-consciousness at being in such an intimate situation with a man she didn't really know.

And yet she wasn't scared. On some fundamental level she totally trusted him—and how crazy was *that*?

'You can get changed in there,' he said, pointing to a small building which resembled a Swiss chalet. 'I'm going up to the house to put on something cooler.'

Lina was relieved when he left, giving her time to compose herself, her relief short-lived when she consulted the full-length mirror and realised how frightful she looked. Hot and bothered and… She unbuttoned her blouse and unzipped her denim shorts and gave a silent groan as she slithered out of panties which felt uncomfortably...*wet.*

And you know why that is, don't you? mocked a taunting voice in her head. *You might be a virgin who has never experienced a scintilla of desire but that doesn't mean you can't recognise it when it comes your way.*

Digging around in her rucksack, she located her swimsuit and pulled it on over her increasingly sticky body, before stepping back to look at the result. Only now the mirror revealed a much too curvy body unflatteringly covered in a plain navy swimsuit and Lina's heart plummeted. What was she even *doing* here?

Slipping from the chalet, she was thankful that Salvatore hadn't returned, though she could see that a tray of coffee had been left on one of the tables. But she wasn't going to hang around for refreshments. She would have a quick swim, get changed and then drive her scooter back home. Go back to where she belonged and forget all her foolish fantasies.

Curling her toes over the edge of the pool, she dived deep into the sapphire waters and a restorative underwater length of the deliciously cool water calmed her fractious nerves a little. Rising up to the surface, she shook her head like a wet puppy, blinking against the sunlight to see Salvatore standing on the side of the pool, and she could feel the painful tightening of her nipples because he was wearing nothing but a pair of bathing trunks.

Exasperation flooded over her. Of course he was wearing bathing trunks! Did she think he was about to go swimming in the black suit he'd worn for the funeral? *So stop staring at him,* she urged herself furiously. *Do some more swimming and then get the hell out of here, back to where you belong.*

But she couldn't.

All she seemed capable of doing was treading water and staring up at him, because he was the most beautiful thing she'd ever seen. His sculpted body gleamed olive in the bright sunshine and his dark, hair-roughened legs were planted firmly on the side of the pool as he stared right back. Lina licked her lips and tasted chlorine but barely noticed it because she couldn't seem to drag her gaze away from him. His broad chest tapered down to a pair of narrow hips and the black Lycra of his bathers was clinging with disturbingly graphic definition to...to...

Lina swallowed, feeling the sudden rise of colour to her cheeks, and swiftly she dived beneath the water again to swim another couple of lengths. But this time the water didn't cool her and when she reached the shallow end of the pool he had slipped into the water and was waiting for her, just as she'd somehow known he would be. He was standing waist-deep, with tiny droplets glittering like scattered diamonds against all that rich golden skin. She wanted him so badly it was as if every atom of her body was longing for him to touch her. Suddenly she understood the reason for all the tension which had been slowly mounting throughout lunch and in the car afterwards. And despite her complete inexperience, Lina knew there was only one thing which could happen now.

If she wanted to.

She looked into his eyes and licked her lips again.

She wanted to.

Did he somehow read her thoughts or was it the hard thrust of her nipples against her navy costume which gave the game away? Was that why his body stiffened, as if someone had just turned him into stone? Lina didn't know and she didn't care, because suddenly it was as if she were being governed by something outside her control—by a force much greater than herself. It was as if she knew exactly what was going to happen, despite her total lack of experience and the laughable inequality which existed between them.

He didn't move—not one inch—but that didn't come as a surprise to her either. She'd somehow guessed he wouldn't.

Because he doesn't really want this, she recognised with a sudden understanding which went way beyond her actual experience. *Oh, on one level he does—on the physical level, for sure. But he's re-luctant to initiate anything he might later regret. He doesn't want to take responsibility for this.*

But she did.

Somehow she knew she needed to.

Which was why she went right up to him and turned her wet face to his, standing on tiptoe and placing her trembling palms on his broad wet shoulders so she could support herself. But mainly so she could touch her lips to his, and kiss him.

CHAPTER THREE

SALVATORE TRIED TO do the right thing. The only thing. Which was not to respond to her in any way. Even though her fingers were digging into his shoulders and her soaking breasts were pressing against his chest. Even though his erection was so hard it felt as if he were about to explode. His throat constricted as he attempted to keep as still as possible and not react, but it was proving almost impossible because he wanted to kiss Lina Vitale more than he could remember wanting to kiss anybody.

He tried to tell himself she was not his type. In fact, she was the antithesis of his type. But that didn't help him much either, because there was something so joyously *vital* about her. Those thick-lashed bourbon eyes. The mass of wet curls, which were streaming in a heavy mass over her luscious curves. It had been the same during the car journey here, when he'd been so achingly aware of her as she'd sat beside him.

How had she managed to do that? He'd barely been able to keep his eyes on the road and when they'd arrived he'd left her to swim, quickly absenting himself in order to rid himself of his erotic thoughts. Alone, in the sane and cool surroundings of his bedroom, he'd thought he'd succeeded in that mission. And then he had seen her rising out of the water like a dark and voluptuous mermaid and—wham. Instant lust had combusted, and now this.

His throat dried because something told him she had the potential to be trouble and he needed to get her out of here as quickly as possible. But then his intentions were detonated by the way she pressed herself closer so that their bodies melded together as if they'd been glued. He could feel the exquisite press of her diamond-hard nipples pushing against the wet material of her swimsuit. Still he didn't voluntarily touch her, just moved his lips so that he could whisper directly into her ear as if someone were listening. But no one was listening. He knew that. He knew it because he'd dismissed the housekeeper and chauffeur for the afternoon so that the place was now empty save for them. Had this been his unconscious agenda—to have a nearly naked Lina Vitale standing compliantly before him, and to be poised on the brink of having sex with her, despite his very real misgivings?

'We aren't going to do this,' he husked, but he

could feel his body tremble as he said it and it felt like a betrayal.

'W-why not?'

'Because…' Pulling away from her ear, he forced himself to look into her eyes and he trembled again, cursing the inexplicable hunger which was heating his blood. He ground out the words with difficulty. 'Because it's pointless.'

'Pointless?'

Salvatore nodded. He'd noticed things about her when they'd been having lunch on the beach. Her trainers had been old and so had her scooter. She was poor and he wasn't stupid. Newspapers regularly highlighted his eligibility. In the race to get him to the altar—which seemed to have been ongoing since he was barely out of puberty—Lina Vitale wouldn't have made it past the starting post, so different was she from his usual choice of sexual partner. And she needed to be aware of that. He needed to destroy any foolish fantasies she might be nurturing before this went any further. He needed to tell her that any kind of shared future was a non-starter.

'I'm leaving tomorrow. And even if I weren't, nothing could ever come of this, Lina, for all kinds of reasons. We're too different, do you understand?'

'I don't care about the differences!' she burst out.

Salvatore narrowed his eyes. He wasn't used to

such honesty and her fervent declaration was chipping away at his resolve. 'If you really want this—'

'I do!'

'If you're absolutely sure about it,' he continued, biting each word out with deliberate emphasis, 'then it's going to be nothing but sex. One night and nothing more. And that's why it shouldn't happen.'

'But what if...?' She hesitated before replying, like someone contemplating the wisdom of their next words, and her soft Sicilian voice was tantalisingly husky as she seemed to draw courage from somewhere deep inside her. 'What if I don't want anything but sex?'

It was the right answer and the wrong answer, all rolled into one. It was like starting a fire and dousing it at the same time. He stroked his finger down over her forearm and felt her shiver. 'You're sure you don't have a boyfriend waiting at home?'

'Quite sure.'

'Or a pack of angry brothers?' he murmured, only half joking.

She pressed her lips together. 'I'm an only child.'

He nearly told her that he was, too, until he remembered that conversation wasn't the reason he was here.

And that was when he kissed her, pulling her into his arms so that he could devour her lips with the hard pressure of his own. He heard her gasp. He very nearly gasped himself and he tightened his grip on her because suddenly this was a kiss like no other. Powerful. Electric. His body shuddered as she thrust her tongue into his mouth in a way which was almost *primitive* but also intensely erotic, as was the brush of her soft belly against him as she circled her hips. Lacing his fingers into her wet curls, he hauled her closer, kissing her for so long that eventually he felt her knees dip, as if she were about to slide to the ground. And that was when he dragged his lips away, hearing her muffled murmur of protest as he did so.

'I want to touch you. To explore this delicious body of yours. Like this,' he husked as he cupped one swollen breast in his palm, and she shivered convulsively. 'Does that feel good?'

'Yes,' she breathed thickly.

He smiled as he peeled the sodden fabric away so that her breasts were bared and bent his lips to first one and then the other, tasting chlorine and salt as he grazed his teeth over each puckered nipple. She gasped again, her fingers curving possessively into his hair, and once again her hips moved in unspoken invitation. He felt the urgent jerk of his erection and the sudden, almost debilitating sense of lust which rushed through his body. Distractedly, he pulled his mouth away from her nipple. He wanted to do it to her here. Now. Maybe on one of those convenient loungers, or maybe in the pool itself with the cool water contrasting against their heated flesh and giving them a space-age feeling of weightlessness. But he didn't have any protection with him and that was something which needed to be addressed, and if he went off to fetch something, mightn't it shatter this incredibly erotic spell?

Placing his hands on her shoulders, he brushed his lips over hers. 'I don't think we're being watched but you can never be too careful and I'd hate to think we were providing some voyeur with a floor show,' he murmured. 'So why don't we go inside?'

Her lips trembled. 'What about…your staff?'

'The house is empty. I gave them the afternoon off.'

She looked as if she was about to ask why, and if she had—would he have told her that, on some subliminal level, maybe he had wanted the house empty in case of just this scenario? But she didn't ask. Just hauled her swimsuit back in place to cover her breasts. 'Okay,' she said.

'Let's go,' he said roughly, linking her wet fingers with his.

Lina could feel her stomach performing flip-flops as Salvatore led her back through the gardens towards the villa. She skirted a large, spiky cacti which lined the path. Now she was out of the water she could feel her skin growing dry, but the warmth of the afternoon sun was having no impact on the goose pimples icing her skin. Her throat tightened as she contemplated what she was about to do. Was she mad? Maybe. She was mad for *him*, that was for sure. He only had to look at her, let alone touch her, and she felt undone. He had tried to talk her out of doing this and maybe that should have been a warning, but in the end—did it really matter? He had been perfectly honest about the temporary nature of this liaison, yet strangely, she didn't care. Wasn't it better that way than if he'd lulled her with lies? If he'd promised to get in touch and then not bothered, wouldn't that be even worse?

As he pushed open the door to the huge house and she followed him inside, Lina realised her conscience was clear. Because who could blame her for wanting this? Bound by a promise she'd made to her dying father, she had stayed with her mother for too long. She had lived a loveless existence for so many years, hidden away in her tiny village and feeling that life was passing her by. She'd never even felt sexual desire before, but now here was the opportunity to experience it for herself. She could find out what all the fuss was about. It wasn't against the law, was it?

Salvatore had paused in the vaulted splendour of the panelled hall and his face was shadowed as he bent to brush his mouth over hers. 'I'd love to give you a guided tour, but I don't think I could give it my full attention at the moment,' he said, the unevenness of his voice betraying an urgency he seemed to be fighting. He tilted her chin so that their eyes met. 'So why don't we just go upstairs? Unless you've changed your mind, of course?'

Lina shook her head. 'No,' she whispered shyly. 'I haven't changed my mind.'

A trace of something like darkness had crossed his features and for one awful moment Lina thought that *he* might be the one having second thoughts. But then his fingers tightened their grip on hers as they ascended a swooping staircase of unimaginable grandeur. Upstairs, a solid wooden door was opened by the impatient thrust of Salvatore's foot to reveal an ancient room. But there was no time to admire the embroidered wall-hangings or the stunning views of the Sicilian countryside as the door swung shut behind them—because Salvatore was pulling her into his arms, undisguised hunger darkening his rugged features and setting up an answering clamour deep inside her. He was stroking damp curls away from her face and his eyes were blazing as he bent to claim her mouth, in a slow and drugging kiss.

And Lina's world tilted, because it was like discovering the existence of a different dimension. She opened her mouth, her fingers kneading the silken flesh at his shoulders, and within seconds she was kissing him back with untutored fervour. For a moment he seemed content with her eagerness and inexperience, before he moved away from her, a touch of impatience darkening his voice.

'Let's get rid of this, shall we?' he ground out, tugging the damp swimsuit over her body and the natural resistance of her undulating hips. 'I want to see you naked.'

It was a masterful command and perhaps Lina should have felt shy as her costume slithered to the ground, since no man had ever seen her like this. But she didn't. She felt strong and powerful as his gaze raked over her, because who *wouldn't* feel good if a man was looking at you with that raw gleam of hunger in his eyes?

Gingerly, he removed his swim-shorts, uttering a low Sicilian curse she was surprised he knew, and Lina felt her cheeks burn as she registered the reason why such a simple manoeuvre had proved so difficult.

'Are you blushing?' he questioned teasingly as he walked towards her. 'And why might that be, Signorina Vitale?'

Lina wondered what he'd say if she told him she'd never seen a naked man before, let alone one who was so obviously aroused. But if she did that then he would guess she was a virgin and she couldn't risk that. Because she wanted this. She wanted this more than she'd ever wanted anything. She didn't want Salvatore reeling back in horror when he realised how inexperienced she truly was. She didn't want him doing the 'right thing'—which she suspected he would—by snapping at her to get dressed and then sending her back to her village. She could just imagine the ride home on her little fifty cc bike, quivering with frustration and humiliation and feeling like a woman who'd been cheated just seconds away from discovering sexual pleasure for the first time in her life.

'It was very hot out by the pool,' she said truthfully.

'And it's going to get even hotter in a minute.' He gave a low laugh of pleasure. 'Come here, *bella*.'

Without warning, he scooped his arm beneath her knees and carried her across the room before placing her beneath the embroidered canopy of the enormous bed. And with that fierce light shining from his blue eyes, Lina really *did* feel beautiful.

He began to stroke her, tracing erotic pathways over her naked skin—only he did it so slowly that it made her want to dissolve with pleasure. Lina swallowed. She was melting! She could feel the heat increasing and the inexorable building of fluttering excitement inside her. She writhed her hips impatiently but still he wasn't making contact with the place where she most wanted to be touched.

'Salvatore,' she whispered, wanting something more without really knowing what it was.

'Mmm?' he murmured, his mouth grazing against her neck so that she could feel the warm fan of his breath, which echoed the rise and fall of his powerful chest. Slipping his hand between her thighs, he parted them before hovering one finger tantalisingly over the sensitive bud of her quivering heat. 'Is this what you want?'

'Yes.' She closed her eyes tightly.

'And this?' he teased as he flicked her a touch.

'Yes!'

His laugh was soft as he began to strum her and Lina almost shot off the bed as he established a soft rhythm. Breathless anticipation captured her in a silken snare as he lured her on towards some unimaginable peak. And suddenly she was falling. Or flying. He shattered her completely, as if he were slowly taking her apart before putting her back together again.

'Yes,' he breathed approvingly and she was aware that he was watching her spasming body with unashamed pleasure. 'I knew you would be passionate from the first time I saw you.'

She thought she must have murmured his name for he gave that satisfied laugh again before reaching out to the nearby table to grab at something—which Lina quickly realised must be a condom. She kissed his bare shoulder as he moved to lie on top of her and his mouth sought hers in a way which suddenly seemed way more intimate than before.

He said: *I want you so much, Lina.*

He said: *You feel incredible.*

And Lina was so dazzled by those words of praise that she touched her fingers to his face in wonder, because even if he didn't really mean them, couldn't she just enjoy being made to feel gorgeous by a man who had fallen into her world like a dazzling star?

And then the fairy tale began to take on a new and unwanted direction. Was it the obvious resistance he encountered as he pushed inside her which made him grow very still? Which made his face darken with something which no longer looked like passion, but a dawning recognition? He uttered another Sicilian curse, one which might have made her blush if she'd heard it anywhere else. But Lina was too concerned about what was happening to worry about profanities. Something much more serious—mainly the very real threat that this might end before it had properly begun.

'You're a virgin?' he verified.

Dumbly, she nodded.

'Why didn't you tell me?'

But Lina wasn't really interested in answering his question—her body was too busy instinctively clenching around the rigid length of him as, softly, he cursed again. But this time his words seemed to lack conviction and suddenly he was moving. Moving inside her. Thrusting up deep into her body and taking on a hard rhythm which felt relentless and incredible. That amazing feeling began to build inside her again and Lina could feel control slipping away as she poised in readiness to take another heavenly flight. Or fall. But it was too late—or too early. Or something. Because Salvatore was choking out a helpless-sounding cry as he bucked within her, sweat sheening his muscular back, so that her own desire shrivelled and died. And when he'd finished there was nothing but the sound of their ragged breathing, which seemed to echo discordantly around the vast room.

CHAPTER FOUR

AT FIRST LINA thought she was alone, mostly because it was quiet. Unbelievably quiet—save for the tweeting of some distant bird. She opened her eyes, aware of nothing other than the tangle of fine sheets and an unfamiliar aching deep in her body. She stretched luxuriously, caught in the dreamy world halfway between sleeping and waking, as fragments of memory came filtering back into her mind. And then she saw Salvatore, silhouetted against the morning sun, which was streaming in through the un-shuttered window beside which he stood. Dark and forbidding and sexy as hell.

And fully dressed.

Now the memory became a sensual stream as she remembered the way it had felt to have him deep inside her. Making her cry out with ecstasy time after time, so that he'd had to kiss her quiet until her body had recovered from that sweet, slow shudder which made everything else seem so insignificant.

Had he heard her stir? Was that why he turned to look at her? She felt her heart turn over as she remembered that time in the middle of the night, when they'd been dissolved by passion and she had felt so close to him. When she had snuggled up against his chest and he'd been stroking his fingers through her hair, and she had confided in him all her dreams that one day she might be able to break away from her mother and make something of herself.

'You're awake,' he observed.

'I am,' she said, trying to keep her voice steady. As though what had happened hadn't been a big deal. And it wasn't, she told herself fiercely. She'd lost her virginity, that was all. She'd spent her adult life wondering whether she'd ever meet anyone who could stir her to the kind of passion she'd only ever read about and now she had. That could be regarded as a positive—just so long as she didn't start having unrealistic expectations about what was going to happen next.

It was a one-night stand, she reminded herself. *It was never intended to be anything else.* And she would be crazy if she ever thought any differently about it.

She smiled. 'You look like you have places to go,

things to do—so please don't let me stop you if you need to be somewhere else.'

Salvatore met her eyes, uncharacteristically unsure of how to respond to her words as a rush of conflicting feelings washed through him. He wanted to tell her, yes, he had to be somewhere else. Somewhere as far away from here—and her—as possible. But that would be tantamount to running away. It would be the action of a coward and he was no coward, even though his head was all over the place this morning. Because Lina *had* been a virgin—something he had suspected even though he'd done a brilliant job of pushing that possibility to the back of his mind. Yet despite her inexperience, she had provoked a seemingly insatiable hunger in him. At times during the night it had felt as if she had cast a spell on him, without his permission. He liked control in the bedroom—as in every other area of his life—and this unsophisticated village girl had temporarily robbed him of that control.

And he didn't like it.

He didn't like it one bit.

'Are you okay?' he questioned.

'I'm fine.'

He shook his head. 'I don't understand,' he breathed, genuinely perplexed. 'Why give me your virginity, Lina? A man you barely know.'

She sat up in bed then and the sheet slipped to her

waist, so that it bared her breasts. Dark curls were tumbling in profusion over rosy-tipped nipples and Salvatore felt the betraying stir of his body.

'I didn't *give* my virginity to you,' she corrected. 'Just like you didn't *take* it from me. It's natural. It's the way of the world and it happens all the time.'

'But clearly not to you. And I fear you may have squandered it with a man like me, who was seeking nothing more than a swift liaison. A pleasant diversion at the end of a tough couple of days.' He sighed, wondering why, after that first time, he hadn't done what he *should* have done and sent her back to her little village. Driven her back in the fading light after she'd freshened up and eradicated the evocative scent of his sex from her skin. Yet she had looked at him with those wide bourbon eyes and he had felt all his resolve slipping away.

'I don't want to go. I want you to teach me,' she had whispered.

'Teach you what?' he remembered whispering back, even though the silken caress of her fingers around the hard jerk of his erection had told him exactly what form her proposed lessons should take.

'About pleasure,' she'd purred.

And he had. God forgive him, but he'd done exactly that. Maybe it had been the heady combination of innocence and appetite which had completely blown his mind. Or the fact that she'd been so eager to learn the things which pleased him. Whatever the reason, he had been suckered in—losing himself in her amazing body, over and over again—until the rose and saffron light of dawn had begun to glimmer on the horizon.

He looked across the room at her as she sat framed against the white pillows, like some fallen Madonna. Her blue-black curls were wild and a rosy flush emphasised the angled slant of her cheekbones and suddenly he wanted her all over again. 'Won't anyone notice that you've gone?' he questioned as, abruptly, he moved a little further away from the temptation of the bed. 'Won't they care that you didn't bother going home last night?'

She shook her head. 'I'm safe. I sent a text to my friend Rosa in the neighbouring village, asking her to cover for me if my mother rang up.'

'Well, you'd better go and shower. Maybe do something with your hair,' he offered critically. 'And then I'll arrange to have your scooter loaded up onto one of the trucks. I can drop you off on the outskirts of your village so you don't have to drive the whole way back.'

'No, really. There's no need. I'm perfectly capable of making my own way home.'

His eyes narrowed, as if he was unused to having his wishes overturned, and Lina managed a thin smile as she pushed aside the rumpled sheets and got out of bed. But her bravado only lasted as long as it took her to get to the bathroom, where she leaned against the door, her heart thumping as she thought: *What have I done?* She stood beneath a terrifyingly efficient shower while powerful jets of water briefly lessened the aching of her body, but nothing could eradicate the painful clench of her heart as she realised that last night hadn't been as straightforward as she had imagined. It was supposed to be about sex and only sex. So why had it felt like something more? Why, when Salvatore had kissed her and stroked and caressed her, had she felt more cherished than she'd ever done before? And it was dangerous to feel that way. She knew that. He'd spelt out word by brutal word that he wasn't looking for anything more.

Raking her fingers through her curls and scrambling into last night's clothes, she returned to the bedroom to find that a tray of coffee had magically appeared. Was his housekeeper back on the premises? she wondered awkwardly as she recalled the unmistakable look of disapproval she'd seen clouding the woman's watchful eyes when she'd arrived.

'Sit down. Have some of this before you go,' Salvatore said as he handed her a delicate cup of the inky brew.

She didn't want to sit down, but she took the coffee and it was delicious. Lina drank down the strong and reviving liquid before picking up her rucksack, and as she straightened up she knew she had to put on the performance of a lifetime.

'Right.' Her smile was bright. 'I think that's everything. It's time I was on my way.'

His eyes narrowed. 'Lina—'

'No.' She would never know where she got the nerve to cut off what sounded like words of regret, but Lina realised it was imperative she didn't slink away, acting as if she'd committed some sort of shameful crime. Because she hadn't done anything wrong. She'd had sex—amazing sex—with a man who had turned out to be a skilled and considerate lover. Surely that was something to rejoice about? He hadn't promised her the stars and she hadn't asked for them. 'You don't have to say anything, because it isn't necessary,' she continued. 'I enjoyed it. More than I ever imagined I would. I've never done anything like this before and I doubt I ever will again. So I'll just say goodbye and let you get on with your day.'

She wouldn't have been human if she hadn't enjoyed the very real sense of discomfiture which briefly darkened his features—as if her words were confusing him. As if he was the one who always called the shots and resented anyone else for daring to take on that role. But what could he say? He certainly couldn't *object* to her dignified departure, could he? She was liberating him from all responsibility and, as a result, Lina felt an unfamiliar sense of liberation herself.

'I'll see you out.'

'Honestly, there's no need. I can find my own way out.'

Some of his steeliness returned as he gritted out his next words. 'I *said*, I'll see you out.'

It felt weird to retrace her steps of the previous night and even weirder to see her little scooter sitting outside the grand villa, with the helmet hung neatly over the handle, looking so sparkly that she guessed the chauffeur must have polished it. But she guessed that was what happened when you were as rich as Salvatore...you just turned your back for a moment or two, and some underling was busy making your world look all perfect and shiny.

'Lina.'

She looked up into his rugged features and saw the sudden darkening of his eyes and for a moment she thought he was about to kiss her goodbye—as if he were offering her some kind of small consolation prize. And something told her that if she allowed him to do that, then all her newfound bravado might just crumble and disappear. Because wasn't her dignity vital at a time like this? Quickly, she took a step back and saw his brow knit together in a frown.

'What's wrong?'

'Your housekeeper is standing behind the shutters watching and she can see everything.'

'I don't care what she can see.'

She thought about the things he'd said. About her having *squandered* her virginity. Why would she want to kiss a man who had delivered such a damning assessment of their night together? Lina crammed her crash helmet down over her curls. 'Well, maybe I do.'

With a feeling close to disbelief, Salvatore watched her walk towards her bike. He'd expected her to hang around until they'd exchanged phone numbers, at least. But instead Lina Vitale was buckling up her helmet as if she couldn't wait to put as much distance between them as possible and, as a consequence, that made him reluctant to see her go, because he was a man who always liked to do the leaving.

He watched as she swung one shapely leg over her little moped and although the denim shorts could in no way be described as revealing, he knew all too well the soft and velvety flesh which lay beneath. Flesh which had been soft and full, like an overripe damson before it dropped to the ground, weighted down by all that sweet, dark juice. He told himself he should be grateful that she had accepted the limitations of their night together with such grace.

But as she twisted the hand-grip of her little

scooter and the engine spluttered into life, he could feel the renewed heat of his blood. And a frustrated beat of longing washed over him as she drove away down the drive, the streaming banner of her hair shining blue-black in the bright Sicilian morning.

'You little *slut*!'

Lina bit her lip. 'Mama, please—'

'What else should I call you when you've just spent the night with Salvatore di Luca?' A truculent jaw was thrust forward. 'Are you going to deny that, Nicolina?'

'I—'

'*And* you lied to me about being with Rosa, didn't you? Or are you going to deny that, too?'

Lina stood completely still as she stared at her furious mother, her heart racing as she tried to piece together her thoughts. She'd known something was wrong from the moment she'd entered the neat little house, her body still warm and tingling with pleasure. She'd been feeling almost *proud* of herself for having walked away from Salvatore's luxury villa so coolly and calmly. For having accepted the status quo. Of course, she wouldn't have been human if there hadn't been a tiny ache in her heart as she'd driven away, because who wouldn't have wanted more? But all those hopeless longings had been forgotten the instant she'd walked in and seen her mother's angry face.

'How did you find out?' she questioned, her cheeks flushing.

'How do you think I found out? I rang Rosa. The friend you were supposedly spending the night with!'

'You *rang* her?' Lina repeated dully.

'Oh, she tried to lie.' Her mother was in her element now. 'To make up some sort of flimsy excuse about why you couldn't come to the phone. But I didn't believe a word of it, and then Sofia Bertarelli confirmed that you'd been with *him*—that you'd turned up there yesterday afternoon, as bold as brass!'

'Sofia Bertarelli?' Lina was puzzled now.

'A customer of mine, who happens to be a cousin of the billionaire's housekeeper!' Her mother spat the words out. 'Whose cousin is a customer of mine and who couldn't wait to tell me!' She clenched her hands, her bony knuckles growing white. 'I can't believe you would behave like that, Lina—like a common little slut! That you would spend the night with a man you barely know and ruin, not just your own reputation, but mine too—as if it hasn't suffered enough already! But it has confirmed one thing. Oh, yes.' A grim look of finality locked her mother's bitter features. 'You won't be leaving this village again until you have had a few lessons in morality.'

Afterwards Lina would wonder what gave her the sudden urge to stand up for herself in a way she'd never been able to do before. Had her first experience of sex liberated her in more ways than she'd thought? Was that why she was able to stare at her mother, not with fear or dread or regret, but with a growing awareness that this was all wrong? That it had been wrong for a long time and she could no longer tolerate it. 'You were checking up on me,' she said dully.

'Of course I was checking up on you—and with good reason, it seems!'

'You have no right to check up on me,' said Lina very quietly. 'I'm twenty-eight years old and I should be free to behave as I wish, just so long as it doesn't hurt anyone. And I haven't.' She lifted her chin very high. 'I haven't hurt anyone.'

But it was as though she hadn't spoken, for her mother raged on. 'You will not leave this village again until I say so! You will work hard and accept your position in life. It's time you were grateful enough to marry a decent man who truly wants you—that's if it's not already too late! But never again must you involve yourself with someone who just takes advantage of your stupidity and lack of judgement by bedding you and then discarding you!'

It was possibly the most brutal thing her mother had ever said, but in a way it spurred Lina on to do something she should have done years ago. But that didn't make it easy. It was never easy to break a pattern which had become so entrenched that you couldn't image a different way of living. 'You can't keep me here by force,' she said quietly.

'Just you try to stop me!'

'No, Mama. I don't think you realise what I'm saying.' Somehow Lina managed to speak quite calmly, even though her stomach was churning. 'I want a change. I *need* a change and I should have done it a long time ago. I've had it with slaving my fingers to the bone and getting no thanks for it. Just like I've had it with you bossing me around as if I'm a child of five, rather than a fully grown woman.' She sucked in a deep breath. 'I'm leaving, Mama. And I'm leaving right now.'

'Oh, really?' Her mother's voice ascended into a shrill shriek as she followed Lina upstairs. 'How am I expected to run the business without you to make clothes for me?'

Lina pulled out an old suitcase and started packing the clothes she'd made to take to her cousin's wedding in Florida, but which had never been used. 'You're perfectly capable of sewing them yourself. Or why not take on an apprentice? There are young girls in the village who will be glad of the opportunity.'

And just see if you can get away with treating

someone else the way you've treated me. But she didn't say that.

'And where do you think you're going to go?' demanded her mother. 'Who on this island do you think will want you?'

Lina snapped the suitcase closed, found her pristine passport and her small stack of savings, then she removed her denim shorts and blouse and wriggled into a clean dress, wishing her mother would give her a little privacy. 'I'm going away. To San Francisco.'

'To be with *him*?' Her mother gave a discordant laugh. 'You think he'll want you now he's got what he wanted?'

Lina shook her head. No. She wasn't that stupid. She didn't think there was going to be some kind of fairytale ending for her and Salvatore di Luca. In the intervening hours since she'd left his bed, he was unlikely to have decided she was the woman of his dreams and he couldn't live without her. But although her billionaire lover had painstakingly explained that he didn't want a relationship with her, he didn't strike her as a dishonourable man and surely he would help her. He owned a plane and was presumably in a position to help her find a job in America. For someone with his wealth and influence, that wouldn't be too big a deal, would it?

After all, it wasn't as if she wanted anything else from him.

Was it?

CHAPTER FIVE

LINA SHIVERED AS the icy look in Salvatore's eyes told her more than words ever could.

She'd known straight away that this was the last thing he wanted—last night's lover turning up on his doorstep and asking him for help. Literally, as he was about to leave. But it was too late to back out now and, besides, what else could she do?

She had been tense with nerves as she had returned to the sprawling villa, terrified he might already have left Sicily and flown back to his home in America. She had arrived in time to see his chauffeur loading smart leather suitcases into the boot of the luxury car, her relief that he was still here soon replaced by the fear that he might not want to see her again. A fear which had been confirmed when Salvatore had appeared at the door of the house and watched her get off her motorbike with suspicion darkening his bright blue eyes. Her heart had sunk as she had looked at his coldly beautiful face because there was no welcoming smile on his lips, nor any kind of greeting to acknowledge the passion they'd shared during the night. Only a cool and steady regard, tinged with a faint but unmistakable impatience. Lina felt like someone who had stepped out of line. As if this wasn't what was supposed to happen and she should have been clever enough to have realised that for herself.

'Lina,' he said carefully, his dark brows raised in arrogant query. 'Did you forget something?'

And Lina knew that if she babbled out an explanation about how a tiny earring belonging to her grandmother, or something equally sentimental, must have slipped down the side of the bed, then a smile of relief would break out on his sensual lips and someone would be instantly dispatched to find it for her. But there was no earring. Nothing had been forgotten or misplaced. She was here to throw herself on his mercy and she tried to think of a diplomatic way to lessen the impact of her request, but there was nothing to fall back on but the unvarnished truth.

'I need… I need your help,' she said.

His blue eyes became hooded. 'I'm not sure I understand.'

Lina tried not to wince at that dismissive response because the subtext to his words was: *This has noth-*

ing to do with me, so please don't bother me with your problems.

She swallowed, twisting a tiny silver ring around her middle finger. 'I need to leave Sicily,' she whispered.

'Your holiday plans are not really my concern.'

'I'm not talking about a holiday.'

'What, then?' he questioned impatiently.

'I was hoping I might be able to ask your advice.'

'About what?'

'About finding a job.'

His powerful body stiffened, like a natural predator which had just heard the crackle of danger, but he flitted her a brief smile, as if the temporary illumination of his handsome face would take the sting out of his next words. 'I'm afraid you're talking to the wrong person,' he said. 'It's true I have a large workforce but I don't micromanage employment issues and, even if I did, I certainly don't take on casual labour on a whim. My human resources team handle that side of my life, so you would need to deal with them. Look, Lina, I don't want to be hurtful, but—'

'No! Maybe I'm not making myself clear.' Her words came tumbling out and she saw his look of surprise, as if he wasn't used to being interrupted. Come to think of it, she was pretty surprised herself—but what was it they said? Desperate times called for desperate measures and she was feeling pretty desperate right now. Didn't matter that Salvatore di Luca was a billionaire and she was a village dressmaker without any formal qualifications, because right now he represented the only hope she had. 'I can't go back home,' she explained. 'My mother has discovered that I spent the night with you and it's the talk of the village. If I stay, she'll make my life a misery.'

His voice was dismissive. 'I'm afraid that's not my problem.'

'I know that. But surely—'

'Surely since I've spent the night with you, it now follows you're my responsibility?' he snapped. 'Is that what you mean, Lina? Even though I specifically asked you whether you were sure you wanted to have sex with me. And you said yes. In fact, you instigated it, as I recall—even though you must have anticipated that you could get found out.'

Lina clenched her fists. She wanted to spill out her hurt at the way he was making her sound so predatory. To tell him he was the most arrogant man she'd ever met and she wondered how she could have fallen into bed with him. But what did she know of the ways of men? Maybe they all acted like this if a woman gave themselves so easily. Wasn't that what she'd been told all through her growing-up years—that a man would lose all respect for you if you had sex with him too quickly? She swallowed, knowing what had happened between them had felt so right—

but that wasn't what mattered now. The only thing which mattered was that she had nowhere to go and she needed Salvatore di Luca on her side.

'Of course I'm not your responsibility,' she answered quietly. 'But my life will be intolerable if I remain here. Surely you can understand that. I'll be seen as a woman of loose morals. I'll be judged every time I walk down the street to buy bread. Have you forgotten what these small villages are like?'

His lip curled. 'I made my escape just as soon as I could. Why didn't you do the same?'

'Because it's different for men, and because I made a promise...' Her voice trembled. 'I made a promise to my father that I would stay and look after my mother, only I've realised it isn't doing her any favours. It's just making her more dependent on me, and it's time she stood on her own two feet. I need to get away, Salvatore—surely you could help me.'

'How?' he demanded, then narrowed his eyes as he appeared to sift through a series of possibilities. 'Do you want to carry on staying in this villa, once I've left? The rental is paid for another week.'

'No. I can't stay in Sicily.'

He gave a slightly impatient flick of his fingers. 'I have a house in Rome you could use.'

Did he really think she could take a flight to the mainland and go to the capital city of Italy, a place where she knew no one? 'That wouldn't work either.' She drew in a deep breath and prayed for courage. 'What I'm hoping is that you could take me to America with you.'

He gave a short laugh and stared at her, as if waiting for the punchline. 'Seriously?'

'All I'm asking is for somewhere temporary to stay until I can get myself settled.'

'Is that *all* you're asking?' he echoed sarcastically.

'I'll pay back any expenses I run-up, I promise you that, even if it takes me the rest of my life. I just need a break, Salvatore,' she finished, on a whisper. 'Didn't someone give you a break when you were starting out?'

Salvatore scowled as her words struck an unwanted chord. Yes, he'd had a break. His godfather had given him enough money to buy an airplane ticket to the New World and to feed himself until he found himself a job.

He knew there was nothing to stop him from telling her she wasn't his problem. From jumping in his limo and roaring away without a backward glance. Her mother might be angry but she would soon get over it—she'd have to. And if the neighbours gossiped, so what? They would only gossip until the next scandal came along. Because she *wasn't* his responsibility. They were both grown-ups. They'd had a one-night stand, that was all.

That was all.

He'd made her no false promises.

He owed her nothing.

Nothing.

But, unerringly, Nicolina Vitale had touched on a raw nerve for Salvatore *did* know how small-town gossip worked. He knew how powerful it could be. How people were quick to judge you, especially if you were a woman. If he turned his back on her now and walked away—wouldn't that be like throwing her to the lions? And wasn't there something about her fervour which made him think of the person he'd been all those years ago—so full of drive and ambition and hope? Was it that which made him hesitate?

'You've never even been abroad and I don't think you understand just how different Sicily and America are,' he argued. 'Culture shock won't come close to it. You don't even speak English.'

'Yes, I do,' she said, instantly switching to that language, admittedly with a rather pronounced Sicilian inflection.

Immediately, Salvatore did the same. 'And just how much of it do you understand?' he questioned imperiously. 'Knowing how to ask the time or get directions to the nearest railway station is one thing. But if that's your standard of fluency, you'll be completely out of your depth.'

She tilted her chin upwards. 'Would you like to test me, then?' she challenged, her voice growing more heated now. 'Do you want me to assure you that I won't make a mistake about "flower" and "flour" and that I know the difference between "angry" and "hungry"?'

Salvatore very nearly laughed and then very nearly pulled her in his arms to kiss the truculent tremble of her lips, because her defiance seemed to have kick-started a slideshow of erotic recall which was starting to heat his blood. Suddenly he could picture her dark olive curves outlined against the white sheet. He could remember how soft she'd felt as she had eagerly opened her fleshy thighs to accommodate his thrusting body. He could recall the sweet tightness as he had broken through her hymen with what had felt like the biggest erection of his life.

'Where did you learn to speak English like that?' he queried unevenly.

'I've always worked hard at my studies and we had a teacher in the village,' she explained. 'A woman from England who fell in love with a Sicilian waiter and came back to Caltarina to be with him. She made it her mission to teach all the children in her care how to speak her mother tongue. She said...' She hesitated. 'She said we never knew when it would come in useful.'

'And maybe she inspired you with more than her language skills,' he suggested silkily. 'Did she also teach you that if all else fails, you can use a man as an escape route from a situation which no longer appeals to you?'

Lina's heart was beating very loudly as his words sank in and she stared at him in growing disbelief. 'Do you think…?' *Say it,* she urged herself, even though it made her feel sick to articulate the insulting implications of his words. She sucked in a deep breath and the air felt hot and raw against her throat. 'Do you really think I slept with you in order to get to America?'

'Who knows?' He shrugged. 'People have done a lot worse to get themselves a Green Card.'

It occurred to Lina that maybe he didn't think so highly of *himself* if he thought she'd targeted him because of that. Surely he didn't imagine that a woman would have sex with him for any other reason than because he was irresistible. But his beliefs weren't her problem. It didn't *matter* what the billionaire thought of her. What mattered was that he gave her a seat on his plane and a temporary roof over her head. Surely that wasn't too much to ask.

'So will you help me, Salvatore? Will you take me to America with you?'

The pause which followed seemed to last for ever until he glanced down at his watch with the slight desperation of the condemned prisoner counting down the seconds to his own execution. 'My jet is leaving in an hour.' His narrowed eyes were shards of unfriendly blue ice as he lifted his gaze to her face and his words were equally cold. 'You can stay on my estate for a few weeks, but no longer. Do you understand what I'm saying?'

'Perfectly,' she said, her heart racing, wondering why, suddenly, he was looking like the enemy.

'Then get in the car,' he snapped.

CHAPTER SIX

IT WAS A day of firsts.

Lina had never been whisked to a private airfield before, or been treated almost like royalty by everyone they came into contact with. As soon as she and Salvatore stepped from the limousine, the tycoon's personal crew flocked around him like fireflies on a summer's night, though she couldn't miss their looks of surprise when they registered that *she* was to be his travelling companion.

Did she look out of place in her handmade dress and the sneakers she'd bought from the local market?

Of course she did, but she couldn't allow such things to bother her. Her position here was nothing to be ashamed of. She wasn't Salvatore's lover. Not any more. That part of their relationship was over. He'd told her very clearly that it was never intended to be anything other than a one-night stand and she told herself she was happy with that decision. She was simply hitching a ride from a man who could help her, and one day she would pay him back in full.

But nerves got the better of her as she fastened her seat belt and she turned to the man beside her, trying not to focus on the long legs which were stretched out in front of him, or the quiet strength which was radiating from his powerful body. 'Do you think we're going to crash?' she asked as he pulled a computer from a soft leather briefcase and the plane's engines roared into life.

He frowned. 'You really think I wouldn't make a point of using the safest planes flown by the best pilots in the business?'

'Then why did the stewardess spend so much time pointing out the emergency exits and showing me how to put on my life jacket?'

He gave a flicker of a smile. 'It's a legal requirement on all flights, Lina. And I hope you're not going to come out with that type of inane comment for the entire journey. Transatlantic travel can be tedious at the best of times, but that would really stretch my patience.'

'I'm sure it would and I'll try my best to keep my *inane* comments to myself. It's just that I've never been in a plane before. I told you that.'

Salvatore stared unseeingly at the blur of figures on the screen in front of him, because that was easier than looking into her dark and smoky eyes. Yes, she had told him. She had told him lots of things but it seemed his hearing had been selective and he'd only registered the things he'd wanted to hear. His fingers hovered over his laptop; for once he was failing to be absorbed by the graphs which dominated the bright square in front of him. Lust had triumphed over reason and, as a consequence, he now found himself in a situation not of his choosing.

'Just read something to pass the time, will you?' he growled. 'Ask one of the crew to bring you some magazines.'

Expelling an impatient breath, he turned his attention back to his computer, because his plan had been to work, just as he always did when he was travelling. He never really stopped working. In interviews, he was often asked why he kept going when his fortune was already so vast, and, although he sometimes brushed the question aside, deep down he knew why. It wasn't just the adrenaline buzz you got while chasing down a tough new deal, or the flush of success when you pulled it off, sometimes against all the odds. It wasn't even the irrational dread which lingered on from his childhood—his determination never to know hunger again.

He narrowed his eyes. No. The reason was far more elemental than that. At least you knew where you were with hard cold dollars and cents. They didn't betray you, or hurt you, or lie to you. It was only people who did that. And it was the people clos-est to you who could tell the biggest lies of all.

An image of painted red lips and nails the colour of blood swam into his mind, accompanied by the mem-ory of a low, taunting laugh. And Salvatore gave silent thanks for being the man he was today. A man who was psychologically self-contained and immune to the wiles of women. He sighed. If only desire could be controlled as tightly as his emotions. His gaze flick-ered across to Lina, transfixed by the way her raven curls tumbled down over the swell of her breasts.

Had he thought he could compartmentalise their explosive night of passion and put it firmly in the past, because to do anything else would be an act little short of insanity? Against his better judgement, he had agreed to provide her with a temporary place to stay, and keeping his distance from her was essen-tial if he wanted to drive home the message that he was unavailable. But maybe he had misjudged her appeal or maybe he'd underestimated how powerful it felt to have his sexuality so keenly awoken after what now seemed like a long time. Because suddenly his work was forgotten. Suddenly Lina Vitale was the sole focus of his attention.

In her simple dress she looked as fresh as a blos-som which had tumbled from a tree—despite the fact she'd had very little rest last night. He could personally vouch for that. Sleep had eluded them both as they had lain with their limbs tangled and, as dawn had washed the bed with warm shades of rose and gold, he had been aware of the olive sheen of her skin, only a couple of shades lighter than his own. There had seemed something indefinably erotic about that. She was the first Sicilian lover he'd ever had—probably with good reason. But reason was the last thing on his mind right now.

He felt his throat thicken as she lifted her head and her lips parted, reminding him of the way she had softly clamped them around his erection in the preceding hours. He wondered if his breath had quickened. Was that why her nipples had started to show through the cheap cotton of her dress?

With an effort, he flicked his gaze back to the screen, but no matter how many emails he tried to compose, the words just kept blurring, because all he could think about was the throb of desire which was hot and heavy at his groin. When she crossed one ankle over the other like that, it seemed like the most erotic action he'd ever witnessed. He couldn't stop thinking about his fingers travelling up her leg to linger on the cool satin of her thighs, or how good it had felt to make that first, tight thrust inside her molten heat. He had taken her over and over again and each time it had felt just as sweet as the first time. Hell, *she* had been so sweet. So openly blown away each time he'd made her come, which had been a *lot*. She had rained kisses all over his lips over and over again, as if she was thanking him. Were all virgins so touchingly grateful?

He didn't want to think about it.

He couldn't stop thinking about it.

His mouth grew dry as the tension between them mounted. It felt as if all the oxygen had been sucked from within the confines of a cabin which had never felt this small before. He was having difficulty breathing and started wondering if the captain had adjusted the pressure. He swallowed.

'So how are the first-time-flyer nerves?' he said, the conversational tone of his question belying the erratic thunder of his heart. 'Feeling a little less anxious now?'

Lina swallowed as she rested her hand on the magazine—the glossy page feeling sticky beneath her hot palm. Less anxious? Was he kidding? She might have had fears about flying, but they had been replaced by a concern about her reaction to him, and the way she couldn't seem to do a thing about it. Did he realise he was making her breasts ache just by looking at her, or that her panties had become embarrassingly damp?

But she wasn't supposed to be thinking about him like that. The brief sexual side of their relationship was a thing of the past—from now on he was nothing other than her reluctant mentor.

With an effort she dragged her mind back to his question and attempted an equally polite answer. 'A bit better, thanks. I think I'm getting used to it. It's certainly a very smooth flight and the clouds outside the window are beautiful.'

The hard glitter of his blue eyes seemed to mock her. 'Are you hungry?'

She shook her head. Was she going mad? Why did she feel as if they were having one conversation, with a whole completely different conversation going on underneath? 'No. Not really.'

'Tired, perhaps? This kind of journey is always draining. There are a couple of bedrooms at the back of the cabin and perhaps you should try to get some rest. The one on the right is quieter. Try that.'

'Good idea,' she said, unclipping her seat belt and rising to her feet. She told herself that sleep was essential. More importantly, it would get her away from Salvatore and the disturbing impact he was having on her senses. He probably wanted to get rid of her. For all she knew, he might be desperate to contact some woman in San Francisco and start arranging to see her the moment he arrived back. And if that were the case then she was going to have to deal with it. He'd made her no promises, had he? He'd offered her no future. And she'd been okay with that. She needed to be okay with that. He was already being generous in providing her with a flight and a home.

If she started wanting anything more, she was risking heartbreak. And she couldn't allow herself to be vulnerable like that—not when she was starting a new life in a new country.

A ridiculous feeling of self-consciousness rippled over her as she picked up her handbag and made her way towards the back of the cabin, wondering if he was watching her. And the crazy thing was that she *wanted* him to watch her—to run that appreciative blue gaze over her in a way which could make her hungry body quiver with longing. But he said nothing more as she left the cabin and Lina quickly went into the bathroom, where she stood for ages holding her wrists beneath a gushing tap. But no amount of cold water was able to bring down her body temperature and eventually she washed her face, brushed out her hair and decided to try and get some rest as Salvatore had suggested. Hopelessly distracted by a head full of erotic images, she walked noiselessly along the softly carpeted corridor and pushed open the bedroom door, her heart missing a beat as she walked in.

Because there was Salvatore.

He had obviously just showered because tiny droplets of water were glittering in the thickness of his jet-dark hair and he was pulling a black T-shirt down over his rippling torso. And he was wearing jeans. Black jeans which hugged the powerful length of his legs. Lina had never seen him wearing anything so casual and he looked almost shockingly sexy. A low curl of heat began coiling itself tightly inside her, round and round and round it went, the pressure building and building with each second that passed. The spring of her nipples began to push almost painfully against the lace of her bra and she wriggled her shoulders a little. It felt as if she were dissolving with desire and she swallowed as she struggled to get the words out.

'I think… I think I may have the wrong room,' she said.

He looked right back at her and the silence which followed seemed to go on for a very long time.

'Not necessarily,' he said, at last.

Lina was no expert when it came to what men wanted, but maybe she didn't need to be. She could see a pulse flickering at his temple and the almost imperceptible tightening of his lips. His smouldering blue gaze and the unmistakable darkening of his eyes were sending out the unspoken message that he wanted her as much as she wanted him. But she had been the one to make the first move last time and since then Salvatore had made it very clear that their relationship was going to be platonic. And wasn't that the best thing? Wouldn't that help to protect herself from the way he made her feel?

She knew what she should do. Squeeze out a polite smile and excuse herself. Find the other bedroom and stay in there until all this inconvenient desire had left her. But she couldn't. And if that could be described as a weakness in her character—Lina didn't care. Because she had spent most of her life being a good girl. Who could blame her if she was enjoying this tantalising feeling of being naughty?

Was that why she just continued to stand there, drinking in his magnificent body with a sexual hunger which was growing stronger by the minute? And suddenly she was getting the distinct feeling that they were each fighting some kind of private inner battle, waiting to see which of them would break first.

It was him.

With something which sounded like a helpless groan, he walked across the cabin towards her and pulled her into his arms, looking down into her face for one long and searching moment—as if seeking the answer she was sure he could read there, before bending his head and blotting out the world with his kiss. And Lina kissed him back. Hungrily. Fervently— dimly acknowledging how different it felt from the first time he'd kissed her. That time it had been all about newness and discovery and his inevitable reaction to her virginity. He had been careful with her, taking his time to extinguish every last bit of apprehension so that she had been bombarded with pleasure, over and over again.

But now he was kissing her in a way which was raw and heightened with untempered passion and suddenly Lina felt more like an equal than a novice. Hadn't he taught her how to enjoy pleasure last night and shown her some of the things *he* liked? So why not show him what an attentive pupil she'd been? Boldly, she slid her hand down the front of his T-shirt, and as she began to massage the hard contours of his torso through the dark material she could hear his slow expelled breath of pleasure.

'Take it off,' he urged her unevenly. 'Undress me, Lina.'

It was empowering to register that note of undisguised need in his voice. But it was nothing but lust, Lina reminded herself as she pulled the garment over his head, though he seemed reluctant to allow her trembling fingers anywhere near his jeans. Quickly, he unzipped her cotton dress and tossed it aside, though he hesitated when he saw her plain white underwear beneath. What was it about that which made his rugged face darken, as if he were having second thoughts? Lina tightened her arms around him and could feel the hard spring of his erection pressing through their clothes, and as he gave what sounded like a soft moan of surrender, everything began to happen very quickly.

Peeling off his jeans, she saw he was naked underneath and very aroused and she let out a gulp of pleasure as he took off her bra and panties and pushed her down onto the bed. Her heart slammed against her rib-cage and already she was at such a pitch of excitement that she couldn't bear to wait for a second longer. Was that why she opened her thighs to give him access to the engorged little bud which he began to strum with sweet accuracy, making her cry out with pleasure, so that he had to kiss her into silence.

'Salvatore,' she moaned, against his lips.

'More?'

She ground her hips against the mattress. *'Yes.'*

His movement became more intense, the position of his fingertip uniquely provocative.

'I've been thinking about doing this ever since you left my bed this morning,' he bit out roughly.

'So have...so have...' But her sentence was destined never to be finished because an orgasm had begun to clench its way through her body and Lina cried out as she began to convulse with the first of those achingly sweet spasms.

The sound seemed to galvanise him into action but he waited until her body was no longer shuddering, before reaching for a condom and stroking it on. And then he moved on top of her and pushed deep inside her, his face dark with fierce concentration. At first, his movements were slow and considered and somehow Lina realised he was waiting for her to have another orgasm before giving into his own. That first fluttering realisation gave way to a heavy beat of expectation, which kept on growing and growing until suddenly her rainbow world was splintering all over again and he was choking out his own gratification.

Afterwards, her arms tightened around him until the sound of his breathing grew less ragged. Tentatively, her tongue flicked out to taste the salt of his skin and she could feel the hardness of one hair-roughened thigh as it lay sprawled over hers. It felt intimate. Intensely intimate—as if they were the only two people in the world. As if all that perfect physicality had forged a special bond between the two of them. As if all the barriers they had both erected around themselves had just slipped away. And somehow that made what had just happened seem perfectly acceptable. Did sex always make you feel like this? she wondered dreamily as she reached out her finger to trickle it slowly down his chest. But her innocent gesture seemed to stir him into action and, even though she could have stayed like that all day, he now seemed determined to move away from her. Suddenly he was rolling onto the other side of the bed and it was as if a giant canyon had sprung up between them.

'Is everything okay?' she asked, before wondering if that was the kind of thing you were *supposed* to say at a time like this.

Salvatore heard the soft uncertainty in her voice and guessed what she wanted. She was probably craving reassurance, keen for him to offer something tangible in terms of a relationship now that they'd been intimate again. But he couldn't do that, and what had just happened should never have happened. He felt a surge of anger, knowing he should have left well alone. He should have blocked out her intoxicating allure, which had reeled him in for all the wrong reasons. He should have sent her away to the other cabin and ignored the urgent throb at his groin which had made him lose control. Because she was wrong on so many counts. Too sweet. Too trusting. Too innocent and untried for a man with his track record of emotional coldness. He would hurt her and he had no right to hurt her, though maybe he wouldn't tell her that. Better she think of him as indifferent, rather than understanding.

Or try to change his mind.

'We need to get a couple of things straight before we land,' he drawled. 'The sex we've just had was amazing, for sure, but it hasn't actually *changed* anything. It was just a moment of physical desire which demanded some kind of release. That's what sometimes happens between a man and a woman. Do you understand what I'm saying?'

'I think I'd have to be pretty stupid not to,' she said.

Salvatore hesitated. He was finding this much harder than he'd expected, mainly because she looked so damned beautiful lying there, her olive limbs sprawled against the sheets with indolent abandon. But he steeled himself against the sudden bewilderment which had clouded her lovely features. 'You're going to be staying in my home and that's something which has never happened before. I like my own space and the idea of a lover being around all the time fills me with dread.'

'I suppose I should thank you for your honesty,' she said.

'I am nothing if not honest, Lina.' He swung his legs over the side of the bed. 'Up until now your life has been protected—by your mother and by the constraints of a small community. But you're going to be living in a big city from now on and you need to learn how to protect yourself. I'm not your guardian and I'm not your boyfriend.' His mouth twisted as he stood up and looked down at her. 'And a naïve young woman clinging to me like a limpet has never been on my wish-list.'

'I have no intention of behaving like a limpet,' she said, with a sudden proud tilt of her chin.

That one simple movement was enough to stir the beginnings of another erection, and Salvatore nearly reached for her again, before stopping himself. Because Lina Vitale could so easily become a millstone around his neck—and that would be way too high a price to pay for the fleeting pleasures of sex.

A chill of awareness whispered over his skin.

She knew no one in San Francisco other than him.

Despite her undeniable sweetness and the lure of her lush body, from now on she needed to be off-limits.

He would provide her with a temporary home, yes. He would ensure she met some of his contacts so she could find herself a job. And once she had gained some independence he could filter her out of his life, for good. He could move her on, having taught her a very important lesson.

That she must never grow to depend on him.

CHAPTER SEVEN

'WE'RE HERE,' SAID Salvatore curtly as the car glided through noiseless electronic gates to draw up in a sheltered inner courtyard.

They had flown into San Francisco—over the iconic bridge and the wide sweep of water which it straddled—before making their way to Salvatore's home. He lived in an area called Russian Hill and Lina thought she'd never seen anywhere quite so affluent. Yet from the outside, the property was relatively unassuming, with tall gates concealing the building from prying eyes. But once those gates had closed she found herself staring up at a modern four-storey building, set in surprisingly extensive grounds, studded with brightly flowering shrubs and heavily loaded citrus trees, which reminded her of home.

'Like it?' Salvatore questioned, his eyes on her face.

She nodded, not terribly interested in his real estate,

but at least it was good to have something to focus on other than the way he had been keeping his distance from her since they'd fallen onto that bed together, high up above the world, in the clouds. Sex on a plane. Nobody could deny that her world was opening up in all kinds of unexpected ways. 'It's beautiful,' she said dutifully.

The front door was opened by a sombre-faced man, wearing a formal dark suit. 'This is my butler, Henry,' said Salvatore.

His *butler*?

'It's good to have you back, Signor di Luca,' Henry said, with a pronounced English accent and the faint semblance of a smile.

'This is Nicolina Vitale, Henry. She's going to be staying here for a few weeks until she's settled in the city. I thought we could put her in one of the vacant cottages. The one furthest from the house might be best.'

'Certainly, Signor di Luca. One of your assistants telephoned earlier and the farthest cottage is already prepared,' Henry answered. 'Perhaps you would care for me to give Miss Vitale a tour around the compound?'

'If you wouldn't mind.' Salvatore pulled his phone out of his pocket and briefly scanned the screen, before shooting Lina an absent-minded look. 'Look, I need to work. Henry will answer any questions you may have and you and I will eat dinner later, as it's your first night here. Eight o'clock, on the terrace. Okay?'

'Thank you,' said Lina, watching him walk away and wondering what on earth she could find to say to the intimidating butler. But she hadn't exactly had much conversation with Salvatore over the past few hours, had she? In fact, their erotic encounter seemed to have created a great space between them. He had treated her with the same polite detachment as he had the stewardesses who had been serving them drinks and food during the transatlantic flight. And Lina had been left trying to focus on that wretched magazine— trying to blot out the aching in her breasts and the memory of him feasting hungrily on her nipples.

She followed Henry through the house and tried to drink it all in, but it wasn't easy for her to get her head around the fact that one man could own a property this big. It was all clean lines and uncluttered space which contained sleek, modern furniture. A space-age kitchen led into not one but two dining rooms, one of which was reached by a glass elevator. The basement housed a carefully lit subterranean art gallery as well as a private cinema, and outside were more seating areas amid tangles of fragrant climbing plants, and a long, cantilevered swimming pool. The highest point of all was the dining terrace, with its sweeping views all the way to Alcatraz and everything in between.

'It's gorgeous,' said Lina politely, though in truth she found it all a little overpowering. 'Have you worked for Salvatore for very long?'

'Five years,' said Henry. 'I first met Signor di Luca at a weekend house party in England when he poached me from the host, and I've been with him ever since.' He gave the hint of a smile. 'He tends to inspire loyalty among his staff.'

'Just how many staff *are* there?' questioned Lina.

'He has a full-time chef and Shirley, who helps out when Signor di Luca chooses to dine at home. And, naturally, there are cleaning staff, gardeners, drivers—the usual kind of thing.'

Lina nodded sagely, as if the concept of personal staff was something she encountered every day of the week.

'Was there anything else you wanted to know, Miss Vitale?'

'No, you've been very helpful. Thank you, Henry. And, please, I'd much rather you called me Nicolina.'

Henry nodded but gave no outward response to her request, other than indicating she should follow him, before leading the way through the grounds to a compact cottage surrounded by trees.

Once the butler had gone, Lina stared out of the window, watching the light beginning to leach from the sky and thinking how surreal this all felt. Because it *was* surreal. One moment she had been living in a village with practically nothing and the next she was staying in the grounds of a billionaire's mansion, being shown around by a butler.

She had no real place here, she realised. Only a temporary one. Just as she had no real place in Salvatore's life. He had seduced her on the plane and she'd let him. Actually, she'd felt herself powerless to do anything else. It had been like a river she'd once seen after the rains, when the water had swollen and banks had burst—flooding everything in its path. And that was what it had been like with Salvatore. That sweet tide of desire had been overwhelming and maybe she needed to think how best to defend herself from feeling that way in the future.

She unpacked her case, then enjoyed a long shower in a bathroom of unspeakable luxury, and, after she'd untangled her curls and dressed, decided to email her mother. They might have parted on bitter terms, but she needed to know that her only child had arrived safely. She switched on her old computer, the glow from the screen dominating her line of vision so that for a while Lina forgot all about Salvatore di Luca and the Californian sky outside her window.

Salvatore walked out onto the wide sweep of terrace and at first he didn't notice her. The light had almost faded from the day and he was preoccupied, as he'd been from the moment he'd arrived at the office, where the staff had seemed surprised to see him working so soon after a long flight. He couldn't blame them because usually he would have spent the afternoon relaxing. He might have swum in the pool or worked out in the gym. But not today—and he knew why. He'd been afraid of running into Lina. Afraid of reliving the way she'd made him feel during the journey from Sicily, when he had felt himself being sucked into that sensual maelstrom despite his determination to resist her. But he hadn't resisted her, had he? He'd allowed her uncomplicated Sicilian beauty to lure him into an unforgettable mile-high encounter—the memory of which he suspected would never leave him.

He'd come home just an hour ago but even a long, icy shower had failed to cool the heat in his blood, and now his attention was caught by the woman sitting on the terrace in front of him, her profile etched starkly against the fiery glow of the setting sun. She was leaning back against a bank of cushions on a low divan, her posture outwardly relaxed as she gazed out at the city view, but her shoulders were hunched with that expectant air of someone who was waiting.

Waiting for him, he thought, and that realisation filled him with an instinctive shiver of disquiet.

She must have heard him for she turned, unable

to hide the quick flash of pleasure in her eyes, which she instantly tried to disguise with a look of polite interest.

'Salvatore! You're back.' She was speaking softly in Sicilian dialect, which itself was disorientating. Was that because it made him think of the past—and of a homeland from which he had been so keen to distance himself? He wanted to tell her to speak only in English, which he knew was unreasonable, yet their spoken bond only added another unsettling layer to his dealings with her. And he wondered yet again what strange sorcery she possessed which was capable of cutting through his habitual iron-hard control.

She scrambled to her feet, the skirt of her cotton dress whispering like a summer breeze, and Salvatore felt a sensation of something unfamiliar as her black curls rippled down around her shoulders. Lust, yes—there was definitely plenty of *that*, along with an instinctive appreciation for her natural beauty, but there was another flicker of apprehension, too. Don't let her get used to this, he found himself thinking. Don't let her think he wanted this kind of cloying homecoming every night.

'Yes, I'm back,' he said smoothly as he ran his finger around the collar of his shirt. 'Did you settle in okay? Did Henry give you the full guided tour?'

'Yes, he did. The tour was amazing and the cottage is lovely.'

Heaven save him from sustained small talk, he thought acidly as he lifted his hand to summon the portly figure of a woman who had silently appeared in the shadows, switching rapidly to English as he spoke to her. 'We'll eat as soon as you're ready, Shirley.'

'Very good, Signor di Luca.'

He half filled two glasses of Gavi and handed one to Lina, but he noticed that she barely tasted the drink, cupping it in her hands as if she'd forgotten she was holding it. It was probably completely unconscious, but in that moment she looked so… *fragile* as she sat there, so clearly out of her depth that Salvatore felt a sudden wave of compassion— and empathy. Because hadn't he once been exactly where she was now? Hadn't he once gazed around at the sumptuous surroundings of billionaire homes and felt as if he'd fallen onto an alien planet?

'So.' He put his glass down on one of the low tables and fixed her with an encouraging smile. 'Did you manage to amuse yourself while I was out?'

Lina nodded as she wrapped her fingers around the cold glass of wine. 'I wrote to my mother and let her know I'd arrived safely and then I started looking online to see what kind of jobs I might be able to find. Soft furnishing companies which need people to sew cushions, or drapes—that kind of thing.'

'And is that what you *want* to do?' He frowned. 'What about all those dreams you talked about?'

She shrugged. 'They don't just happen.'

'Couldn't you make them happen?'

Lina swirled her wine around in her glass. It was so easy for him to talk. What would he say if she confessed she was terrified her ambitions might wither under the brightness of the Californian sun? 'I have to have some money coming in first,' she said. 'And then I'll see. I have savings, but I'm going to be very careful about how I spend them.'

'Well, that sounds like a very sensible plan.' His voice was grave but she could see the faint upward curve of his lips. Was he inwardly laughing at her? she wondered.

But Lina pushed aside her concerns as she sat down at the table, determined to enjoy her dinner. The meal began with a creamy fish soup, which Salvatore called chowder, followed by a fillet of perfect fish, served with its own little jug of sauce. She tucked into every course with a keen appetite, putting her dessert spoon down at the end to find Salvatore studying her, with what looked like amusement sparking from his narrowed eyes. 'It's good to see a woman who enjoys her food,' he observed.

'I was hungry.'

'I could see that. Don't look so defensive. I meant it. Most women order a plate of rabbit food and then just pick at it.'

'That's why they stay so slim.'

'Don't ever think you don't have the perfect body, Lina,' he said softly. 'Because you do.'

It was like a rock being dropped into a still stretch of water—the relative calmness of the meal disrupted by the sudden violent splash of memory. Powerful and erotic memory. Silhouetted against the glittering backdrop of the city, Lina thought how unbelievably virile the tycoon looked in a shirt the colour of an oyster shell—the silky material emphasising his broad shoulders. It was weird to think they had been eating their meal so primly when just hours ago he had been deep inside her body. Yet his words were unexpected and they changed the atmosphere completely. His quiet praise made her feel almost confident. Was it that which made her ask the question she'd been longing to ask him all day?

'Do you think you'll ever go back to Sicily?'

His voice was repressive, his powerful body tense as he put his coffee cup down. 'I doubt it.'

Lina pushed her dessert plate away. Okay, so he didn't want to talk about Sicily—but they had to talk about *something*, didn't they? Otherwise every time she ran across him she was going to feel increasingly agitated.

Focus on something other than the curve of his lips and the carved contours of his face, she told herself fiercely. *Ask him something easy.*

'Where are your parents?' she asked suddenly.

Almost imperceptibly, his knuckles tightened. 'Why do you ask?'

'It's a normal question. Nobody in the village knew anything about them. Apparently your godfather never talked about them, even when he was well. I was just thinking how proud they must have been of your success.'

Salvatore stilled. Funny how a guileless statement like that had the power to tug you back towards a darkness and a past he tried to keep out of bounds. 'My parents never got to see it,' he said coolly. 'They were dead by then. They died a long time ago. Long enough for everyone to have forgotten about them.'

'I'm so sorry,' she said quietly. 'What happened to them?'

There was a pause and Salvatore felt a flicker of irritation. Didn't she realise from his tone that he didn't want to talk about it? That over the years he had built a high wall around his emotions? An impenetrable barrier, which discouraged investigation into his past—a concept easily accepted by a culture which was keen to live in the moment. But Lina Vitale was looking at him with such genuine compassion shining from her eyes that Salvatore felt some of his usual resolve melt away.

Was it because she was Sicilian and they were speaking quietly together in dialect that he found himself wanting to break the most fundamental of his self-imposed rules and talk to her on a level he never usually engaged in with other people? Or because she looked so damned lovely that he needed to distract himself from giving in to what he most wanted to do—which was to carry her off to his bedroom and ravish her over and over again, until she was shuddering out his name and biting her little white teeth into his bare skin?

And he wasn't going to do that any more. He'd demonstrated quite enough powerlessness around her. He needed to claw back some of the control which had so disturbingly left him on the plane today.

But she was still looking at him and something about her soft gaze was making him want to spill it all out. And why not? It wasn't as if he *cared* about what had happened in the past, was it? Not any more. He had schooled himself to ensure he didn't really care much about anything, or anyone. A brief explanation might provide a welcome diversion from the rise and fall of her breath, which was making her luscious breasts move provocatively beneath her dress. And mightn't talking about it prove to him—

self once and for all that the past no longer had the power to hurt him?

He swallowed the last of his wine and put the glass down. 'My father was a fisherman, though not a particularly effective one,' he began, arching her a questioning look. 'You know what they say about fisherman's luck?'

She shook her head. 'Not really.'

'Getting wet and catching no fish,' he explained, with a rare flash of black humour which made her smile. 'As a consequence we had very little. We were among the poorest in one of the poorest villages on the island. The bottom of the heap, if you like. And it made my mother...discontented.'

She didn't say anything. If she had, he might have clammed up. But as her silence washed over him with purifying calm, he found himself continuing.

'A life of poverty wasn't what she had signed up for. She was a beautiful woman who had always attracted the attention of men and that made my father jealous. Jealousy is an ugly trait,' he added, his mouth twisting. 'I could hear him shouting at her at night-time, when I was trying to sleep. He used to accuse her of flirting. Of wearing clothes which were too tight and lipstick which was too red. Sometimes their rows were so loud they used to wake up the neighbours and all the local dogs would start to bark. And she used to taunt him back. She told him he couldn't even provide for his family. She said he wasn't a *real* man.' He gave a bitter laugh. 'Living with them was like watching a never-ending boxing match, with each one circling the other, waiting to make the killer blow. Like having a bomb ticking away in the corner of the room, just waiting to go off.' It hadn't felt like life, it had felt like *existence*— a claustrophobic prison from which he'd been unable to escape and which had soured his appetite for close relationships in the years which had followed.

'Go on,' she said, in a voice so soft it was barely audible.

He drew in a deep breath, surprised by the ease with which he was saying it, as if someone had sweetened a mouthful of poison and made it almost palatable. 'One day, when my father was out on his boat, a travelling salesman came by the house—a slick stranger who seduced her with the promise of silk stockings and a better life. By the time I got home from school she had already packed her things and was getting ready to drive away in his fancy car.'

He was lost in the past now; he could feel it sucking him back into a great gaping vortex of darkness. His mother had crouched down and told him she would send for him just as soon as she was settled but something inside him had known she was lying. He would never forget the kiss-shaped mark of lipstick she'd left behind on his cheek, which he

"One Minute" Survey

You get **TWO books** <u>and</u> TWO Mystery Gifts...

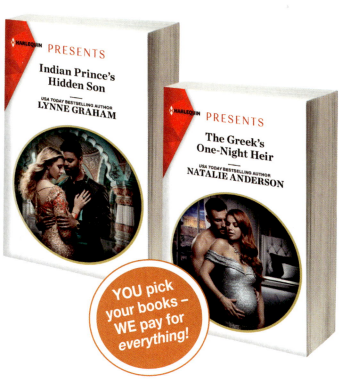

HARLEQUIN PRESENTS

Indian Prince's Hidden Son

USA TODAY BESTSELLING AUTHOR
LYNNE GRAHAM

HARLEQUIN PRESENTS

The Greek's One-Night Heir

USA TODAY BESTSELLING AUTHOR
NATALIE ANDERSON

YOU pick your books – WE pay for everything!

See inside for details.

YOU pick your books –
WE pay for everything.
You get TWO new books and TWO Mystery Gifts…
absolutely FREE!
Total retail value: Over $20!

Dear Reader,

Your opinions are important to us. So if you'll participate in our fast and free "One Minute" Survey, **YOU** can pick two wonderful books that **WE** pay for!

As a leading publisher of women's fiction, we'd love to hear from you. That's why we promise to reward you for completing our survey.

IMPORTANT: Please complete the survey and return it. We'll send your Free Books and Free Mystery Gifts right away. **And we pay for shipping and handling too!**

Thank you again for participating in our
"One Minute" Survey. It really takes just a minute *We pay for EVERYTHING*
(or less) to complete the survey… and your free books and gifts will be well worth it!

Sincerely,

Pam Powers

Pam Powers
for Reader Service

"One Minute" Survey

GET YOUR FREE BOOKS AND FREE GIFTS!

✓ **Complete this Survey**   ✓ **Return this survey**

1 Do you try to find time to read every day?
☐ YES   ☐ NO

2 Do you prefer stories with happy endings?
☐ YES   ☐ NO

3 Do you enjoy having books delivered to your home?
☐ YES   ☐ NO

4 Do you find a Larger Print size easier on your eyes?
☐ YES   ☐ NO

YES! I have completed the above "One Minute" Survey. Please send me my Two Free Books and Two Free Mystery Gifts (worth over $20 retail). I understand that I am under no obligation to buy anything, as explained on the back of this card.

❏ I prefer the regular-print edition
106/306 HDL GNPG

❏ I prefer the larger-print edition
176/376 HDL GNPG

FIRST NAME

LAST NAME

ADDRESS

APT.#

CITY

STATE/PROV.

ZIP/POSTAL CODE

had scrubbed afterwards until his skin was red raw. Or the way the salesman had looked right through him, as if he were invisible—a tedious little obstacle which had been put in their path. His father had erupted with a heartbreak which had made the young Salvatore flinch with shame. Crying big savage sobs, he had thrown himself down on his knees in front of his straying wife, his shoulders shaking as he'd begged her not to go.

But she had. She and the salesman had driven away in a cloud of dust. And Salvatore had been left with his father's grovelling display in front of the small crowd who had gathered there. Just as he'd been left with his own sense of confusion and outrage. In that moment he had recognised the humiliation that women could heap upon men, and how a man could let his obsession for a woman make him lose his mind. He had never forgotten either of those lessons. And he had been right about his mother's lie, because she had never sent for him, despite the promise she had made. 'My mother and her lover were killed in a car crash the following year,' he added grimly. 'And soon after that, my father was lost at sea.' He gave a bitter laugh. 'They called it an accident, but I never considered it one, for he lost the will to live after her desertion.'

'Oh, Salvatore.' Her voice trembled and he

could hear the soft note of tenderness in her voice. 'That's…that's awful.'

He shook his head and held up his palm. 'Platitudes are not necessary, Lina,' he said, hardening his heart to the way she was looking at him, as if she wanted to cradle him in her arms and take away all those bitter memories. And *that* was why he didn't ever talk about it, he reminded himself grimly. He would not be seen as a victim. As someone to be saved, or pitied, or rescued. Because he'd managed to mastermind his own rescue and he'd done it all himself. 'I didn't tell you because I wanted your sympathy.'

There was a flicker of a pause. 'Then why did you tell me?'

'Maybe I just wanted to make it clear what has made me the man I am. To make you understand that I mean it when I say I don't want any long-term emotional commitment. Perhaps now you can understand why.'

'Because you don't trust women?'

'No.' He shook his head. 'Because I know my own limitations. I just don't have the capacity to care, Lina—or the willingness to do so. I've always been that way and that's the way I like it.'

He saw the clouding of her eyes just as his phone began to vibrate on the table and he snatched it up, glad of the interruption. He listened intently for a few moments before terminating the call and rising to his feet, his heart twisting with something inexplicable as he looked down into her big, dark eyes. 'I need to deal with this call and then I'm going to turn in for the night,' he said abruptly. 'But stay as long as you like and ring for anything you need. Shirley can get you coffee—'

'No. I mean, thank you, but no.' With a fluid movement she rose from the table. 'I'm tired too and I'd like to turn in.' She hesitated. 'I don't suppose you'd show me the way? This place is so big I'm terrified of getting lost.'

The last thing he wanted was to escort her back in the seductive light of the moon. To imagine the bed which lay within the little cottage and think how good it would feel to sink down on it with her in his arms and to lose himself in her sweetness. The spiralling tension which had tightened his groin into an exquisite ache made him want to refuse her innocent request, but wouldn't that imply that he couldn't trust himself around her?

He stayed silent as they walked through the grounds, trying to concentrate on something other than the whisper of her skirt in the light breeze and the way it swayed over her curvy buttocks. But as she stopped in front of the door, with the scent of flowers heavy and potent in the night air, and the black curls streaming over her thrusting breasts, he felt a rush of desire so powerful that he almost succumbed to it.

It would have been so easy to take her into his arms and kiss her. Too easy. Despite everything he'd said on the plane, he was beginning to realise that resisting Lina Vitale might not be as simple as he'd thought. Would it hurt to retract his words? To override his original intentions and give into the most powerful sexual attraction which had ever come his way? Surely it was insane to deny them both what they wanted, when this kind of physical chemistry was so rare.

He swallowed. Maybe, at a later date—when he was certain she could accept his boundaries and his limitations. Because if—when—he had sex with her again, it would be at a time of *his* choosing. When he was certain Lina understood that *he* was the one in the driving seat. The one with all the control. He would make himself wait, because not only would it increase his hunger, it would prove he didn't need her. Maybe the time would come when they could be friends with benefits, yes, but it could never be anything more. And in the meantime, he needed to ensure she had some kind of focus other than *him*.

He stopped outside her doorway and looked at the moonlight-dappled darkness of her hair. 'One of my charitable foundations is giving a gala ball tomorrow night,' he said. 'Why don't you come along?'

'You mean, as your guest?'

Deliberately, he downplayed it. 'Why not? You'll get a chance to meet some people. Contacts which may come in use, if you're going to start looking for a job. You might actually find something to do with your life which is a little more exciting than sewing drapes and curtains. Isn't that what you came here for?'

'Yes, yes. Of course it is. It's just that...' She hesitated as she fingered the flared fabric of her dress before lifting her gaze to his. 'I've never been to a ball before.'

'I don't imagine they're a big feature of life in Caltarina,' he said drily.

'Which means I don't have anything suitable to wear,' she continued. 'And there won't be time for me to make anything suitable.'

'No problem. I can buy you something.'

'That wasn't what I meant, Salvatore. I can't possibly let you do that. You've already been more than generous.'

'The subject isn't up for debate' he said coolly. 'I can afford it and you can't. You can add it to the list of things you say you're going to pay back.'

'I say it because I mean it!' she clarified fiercely. 'I'll pay back every cent.'

He gave a slow smile, because in that moment she reminded him very much of himself. 'Okay. Now go and get some sleep,' he said softly. 'It's been a long day.'

He turned and walked away and Lina watched him, still trying to absorb everything that had happened. He'd told her about his childhood, which had made her heart bleed for him. Things which had made her want to wrap her arms around him and comfort him and try to take some of his pain away. She bit her lip. Her own mother might have been stupidly strict, but at least she'd *been* there for her. And Salvatore's face had looked so stern as his story had unfolded, his troubled features shadowed by the flicker of candlelight. He had obviously intended to convince her that the past no longer had the power to affect him, but Lina had detected the faint dip of vulnerability in his voice. She had seen the ravaged expression which had darkened his face when he'd described his mother driving away in the salesman's car. And she had died before they'd had an opportunity to resolve their broken relationship. Of *course* it must still hurt, no matter how hard he tried to deny it to himself. She suspected he'd buried it away so deeply that he'd never really allowed himself to grieve.

And his father had left him, too. So wrapped up in his own bitterness and heartache, he had neglected the little boy who must have been missing his mother—and, in so doing, had managed to destroy yet another area of trust.

Stepping inside, she shut the door behind her, leaning heavily against it and closing her eyes. Had she thought he might kiss her when he'd walked her to the moonlit cottage? Yes, she had. Of course she had. And even though she was starting to realise that she couldn't just keep being *available* whenever he snapped his fingers, she couldn't deny that she wanted him.

But she couldn't afford to behave like a passive puppet around this undeniably sexy and charismatic man, because she had come to America to make something of herself.

Not to get her heart broken.

CHAPTER EIGHT

THE KNOCK ON the cottage door sounded imperious and Lina felt a ripple of apprehension as she opened it to find Salvatore standing there, his muscular physique dominating the star-sprinkled sky behind him. And despite all her intentions to do otherwise, her heart began pounding frantically beneath the fancy fabric of her new dress.

It was a little under twenty-one hours since she'd last seen him. Twenty-one hours of trying to get to know some of the staff a bit better and asking Henry if there was anything she could do to help. Answer: no. In theory, twenty-one hours to build up some immunity against the charismatic tycoon. So why hadn't it worked? All the stern talking-tos in the world didn't seem to have changed her body's instant response to him, which was as powerful as ever.

It was as if she'd been stumbling around in the dark for a long, long time and Salvatore had suddenly become her bright, hard focus. Whenever he was around her skin felt sensitive—her limbs weightless and her senses soft. It was as if the very substance of her was capable of dissolving whenever he was in the vicinity.

He flicked his gaze over her and Lina wondered if she'd imagined the brief flash of disbelief in his eyes. She doubted it. Hadn't she experienced a similar reaction when she'd stood in front of the mirror a little earlier and surveyed the image reflected back at her? She shifted her weight on her stiletto heels because she was doing everything she could to avoid getting a blister this evening. She wasn't used to wearing an evening dress, nor shoes this high, and as she waited for Salvatore's verdict on her appearance her already jangled nerves felt even more frazzled. It was exactly as she'd thought. She looked a disaster. She was going to let him down. She would turn him into a laughing stock. 'You don't like it?' she said.

There was a pause as he continued to study her with an unhurried scrutiny which was making her nipples tighten.

'You look *different*,' he concluded eventually.

It wasn't the reply she'd wanted but maybe it was the only one which was appropriate. Because she felt different. She felt… Lina shook her head, but not a single hair of her perfectly coiffed head moved, thanks to the careful ministrations of the in-store hairdresser. It was difficult to describe exactly how she felt. Disorientated might be a good place to start. She'd never been to an upmarket department store before, nor been assigned a personal shopper—but apparently this was perfectly normal when you possessed the platinum store card to which she'd been given unfettered access by Salvatore di Luca. But nothing could have prepared Lina for the lavish interior of the sumptuous San Franciscan store, nor the expensive outfits of her fellow customers, who glided over the marble floors as if they had been shopping there all their lives. Never had she felt quite so poor or provincial.

Her relief at being given guidance by the personal shopper was tempered by the realisation of how many of the dresses—which all looked remarkably similar—she was expected to try on.

After countless hours she ended up with a simple floor-length robe in cobalt-blue—which wasn't her usual style *or* colour, but which she was assured made her look *stunning*. The shopper had arranged for a make-up artist to apply unfamiliar cosmetics to Lina's face and, in the brand-new and restrictive underwear which was containing her curves beneath the dress, she felt like a sausage about to burst out of its skin. She was dressed up like a painted doll in an expensive dress so narrowly cut that she had to take ridiculously tiny steps in order to walk.

Salvatore was still looking doubtful.

'I'm not sure it suits me,' she said, thinking that the same thing certainly couldn't be said for him. With a dark dinner jacket clinging to his broad shoulders and impeccably cut trousers emphasising the length of his powerful legs, the Sicilian tycoon looked cool, handsome and impossibly inaccessible.

'You *don't* like it,' she continued when he failed to contradict her, her hands falling to her sides and brushing impatiently against the heavy material.

'I didn't say that. You look chic and sophisticated,' he amended smoothly. 'Wasn't that supposed to be the whole idea?'

'I guess so,' she said, but suddenly Lina felt like a fool. In principle the idea had seemed so simple—in reality, less so. Buy a poor girl a fancy dress and then take her to the ball. Why hadn't either of them stopped to consider that a Cinderella-type transformation might not work in her case, since the raw material was too rough to ever be properly smoothed off at the edges?

He glanced at his watch. 'Since we're already fashionably late and the car is outside, we really ought to leave. Are you ready?'

She shook her head. 'No. I've changed my mind. I don't want to go. You go without me. You'll have a better time.'

'Falling at the first hurdle?' His blue-hued gaze

was direct and mocking. 'I thought you were made of stronger stuff than that, Lina. Or have you had a sudden personality change from the woman who begged me to take her to America so she could start a whole new life? Isn't this what you wanted?'

On one level she was aware he was goading her, but somehow it worked. Because what else was she going to do, if she pulled out? Hang around the estate all evening and risk annoying Henry, or ruffling the feathers of the chef, who wasn't expecting either of them to be home this evening?

'It's true. I can't back out now.' She drew in a deep breath. 'You're right.'

'I nearly always am.'

His arrogance almost made her smile and, ignoring the matching cobalt clutch bag which the in-store dresser had insisted on foisting upon her, Lina grabbed one of the embroidered velvet bags she'd brought with her from Sicily. With its distinctive beading and flouncy tassel, it was obviously home-made and didn't particularly match the severe dress she was wearing. But at least it was *hers*—she had made it herself— and right now it felt like the only authentic part of her appearance.

The waiting limousine purred them through the steep streets until they reached a luxury hotel, not far from the glittering waterfront. Soaring up into the starry sky, its floodlit pillars reminded Lina of a

Grecian temple she'd once seen in a book. Outside, thick scarlet ropes kept back hordes of onlookers brandishing cell phones, and the whole scene was illuminated by the bright flash of paparazzi cameras.

She could feel herself freezing, wondering how on earth she was going to get out of the car in front of such a massive crowd of people. Her legs were so wobbly that, once again, she was paralysed by fear. She shook her head. 'I can't go in there,' she husked.

'I thought we'd already had this conversation,' he said, not bothering to hide the boredom in his tone. 'Of course you can.'

'My heels are too high.'

'They look pretty good to me.' She saw the glint of something vaguely unsettling in his eyes as he focussed his gaze on her footwear. 'You can hold onto me if you're worried about your balance.'

'Salvatore, you don't understand.' Lina clutched the handle of her little velvet bag. 'I've never been anywhere like—'

'I understand better than you think.' He cut across her words. 'Don't you think I've experienced exactly what you're going through right now, Lina? Or do you imagine I was admitted to these types of glittering affairs with open arms? That society matrons didn't feel they had to lock up their daughters whenever I put in an appearance, while their billionaire husbands nervously watched their backs in case I deposited a blade in between their shoulder blades?'

'Did they?'

'Yes, they did. They saw me as a threat.' His mouth twisted into a grim smile. 'Because I was. My hunger to succeed made me ruthless and my determination to escape the shackles of my past drove me on. I wouldn't let anything stand in my way to get what I wanted.' There was a flicker of a pause. 'Can't you try and do the same?'

Lina shook her head. 'That's easy for you to say. People don't judge you on your appearance or whether you can walk straight in a pair of shoes so high you feel as if you're on stilts. You're a man.'

'Then don't *let* yourself be judged,' he urged. 'Wasn't that one of the reasons you left Sicily? Don't forget how much you wanted to get out of there. It's not going to work for you unless you're prepared to be brave.'

It was difficult to think of bravery when he was sitting so close to her, making things more complicated than they needed to be. She thought how much simpler it would be if she hadn't had sex with him. Wouldn't that have made it easier to concentrate on what lay ahead, rather than on the tingling sensation that his hard thigh was mere millimetres away from hers?

'Maybe I should just have stayed where I was in Caltarina and ridden out the storm,' she said.

'And done what? Carried on slaving away doing something you didn't really like, for a woman who took you for granted? Squandering your youth and your beauty while the years passed you by?' Suddenly he put his hand on her forearm, but with the impersonal touch of a dentist patting a child's arm and reassuring them that it wasn't going to hurt. 'You don't have to do that any more, Lina. You have a chance to make something of yourself here. A career, most certainly, if you're prepared to work. And a husband, perhaps, in time. Isn't that what most women of your age want? Some all-American boy who can provide you with the white picket fence and roses round the door.'

Lina could tell he was trying to reassure her and supposed she should feel grateful for that, but the stupid thing was that his words *hurt*. They hurt far more than they should have done. She turned her head to stare fixedly out of the window, blinking furiously, terrified by the sudden threat of incipient tears. How dared he talk so casually about the husband she might or might not one day have, as if he didn't care about her? To paint a picture of a future which most definitely didn't include him?

Because he doesn't care.

He'd made that clear. Right from the start.

He had told her very definitely she was not what he was looking for. That no woman could give him what he wanted other than sex. So maybe it was time she started believing him.

She drew in a deep breath. 'Okay. You're right. Let's go in. I'm ready now.'

'Take my arm.'

She hesitated. 'I'm not—'

'Take it,' he interrupted impatiently. 'Anything is preferable to spending the night in the emergency department if you're genuinely afraid of tripping over on those killer heels.'

That *did* make her smile, and she nodded. 'Okay. Thanks.'

But Salvatore could feel the nervous pressure of her fingers as they ascended the marble stairs leading into the famous Westchester Hotel, in a flurry of flashbulbs. He didn't know why she was so worried about her appearance, not when she looked so arresting. In fact, he'd barely recognised her, and not just because her hair had been intricately fashioned on top of her head, drawing his attention to her delicate profile and the graceful line of her neck. He'd found himself thinking that the style was light years away from the billowing curls which had flowed from beneath her dusty crash helmet as she had ridden away in the Sicilian sunshine. That young woman had been replaced by a sophisticated socialite with darkened lashes and provocatively gleaming lips. He'd never seen her wearing make-up before, just as he'd never seen her voluptuous body sculpted in a way which seemed to have made her exceptional curves disappear. She no longer looked like the vibrant woman he had seduced—more like an identikit version of the type of partner who usually graced his arm.

Did that make her more or less desirable? He couldn't quite decide. It certainly made her seem more...*manageable*.

He could hear the ripple of interest from the milling crowd as they entered the ballroom and every head in the place turned to look at them, though that came as no surprise. His appearance at this kind of events always excited fascination—though never more so than when he had a new woman in tow. The press were always trying to marry him off—as were the matrons who had once spent so much time trying to shield their daughters from him. Yet there hadn't been a woman on his arm for a long time. There had been speculation that his heart had been broken or that he was conducting an affair with a married woman, but neither of these were true.

The reason for his lack of a partner he put down to a growing cynicism about the way his fortune impacted on those around him, especially women. It had at first made him feel deeply uncomfortable, and then to grow exceedingly bored by the predictability of it all. He'd discovered that as his wealth grew, so his lovers had started going out of their way to accommodate him. To be understanding and undemanding. They made sure they were up to date on current affairs and knew a healthy amount about his various businesses. He'd noticed too that they became increasingly daring in the bedroom—or out of it. No matter how high-powered their working lives, at the end of the day they'd all seemed cast from the same mould. They suggested newfound erotic diversions alongside their determination to craft the perfect *mille-feuille* pastry, as if by combining all these attributes and presenting them to him in a sleek and very sophisticated package it would make them the perfect wife material.

But he wasn't looking for a wife. He never had been. To him, marriage had always seemed something to avoid. And even though some of his best friends had recently succumbed—Lucas Conway and Matteo Valenti being two cases in point—Salvatore's fixed stance on matrimony hadn't altered. He suspected that his distrust of women had been the reason why he'd been so susceptible to a brief fling with someone like Lina—a simple country girl who seemed to possess no airs or graces. That night with her had been the first time in a long time that he'd felt control slipping away, and it had disturbed him. And he had succumbed to her again during the flight from Sicily, despite his determination to resist her.

But he had clawed back that temporary loss of control, hadn't he? He hadn't kissed her after dinner last night, despite his overwhelming desire to do so. He had concluded that maybe he would wait a little longer before he made love to her again, but when he'd called for her tonight and seen her dressed up and ready to go out, his resolve had wavered, big-time.

He wanted her.

He wanted her now.

'Salvatore?'

Lina's soft Sicilian accent broke into his thoughts and Salvatore focussed his attention on the fractured light from one of the chandeliers which was painting rainbow hues over the dark coils of her hair.

'What?'

'Is that Siena Simon over there?'

He glanced across the ballroom in the direction of her gaze, where a glamorous woman in a pale dress was surrounded by an adoring group of younger men. 'Yes,' he said absently. 'What of it?'

'Gosh.' Lina felt a flare of disbelief as Salvatore confirmed that one unbelievable fact—because the world-famous American dress designer had long been a hero of hers. Everyone in Sicily went wild

for SiSi clothes, though not many people could afford
to buy the real thing. 'I'd love to meet her.'

Salvatore flickered her a brief smile. 'Then why
don't you go up and say hello?' he suggested softly.

'I can't just walk over there and introduce myself!'

'Why not? You can do anything you set your heart
on. It's called networking and it's what you have to
do if you want to get on in the big city. Go on.'

His tone was weirdly encouraging but Lina's heart
was in her mouth as she walked across the ballroom
and hovered nervously on the edge of the circle until
one of the flamboyant young men noticed her and
drew her in. And that was when she was introduced
to Siena Simon. Clad in a sculpted cream gown, the
international designer was gracious as she extended
her hand, though her gaze kept flickering to the little velvet bag which was dangling from Lina's arm.
And even though Lina wasn't sure if it was a good
idea, she found herself confiding that SiSi clothes
were the most popular rip-offs on Sicilian market
stalls, and Siena actually laughed.

'That's good to know,' she murmured, in her soft
American drawl. 'And don't they say that imitation
is the best form of flattery?'

After that, her confidence boosted, Lina met
loads of people. To her surprise, the evening passed
in a blur of chatter, champagne and a very fancy
dinner—during which she was seated between an

Australian entrepreneur and an actor called Sean
MacCormack, who was apparently a big star on a
daytime soap she'd never even heard of. At first she
was so nervous she could barely get a word out and
terrified that her Sicilian accent would make her difficult to understand. But both men were absolutely
charming, and Sean told her she was welcome to go
and watch him filming any time she wanted. When
dinner ended, the band began to strike up a tune at
the far end of the ballroom and Lina's heart gave a
predictable punch of excitement when Salvatore returned to her side.

'Can we go now?' she asked him.

He seemed surprised. 'Are you sure? The dancing is about to start.'

'I know that.'

'So let's dance.'

'I thought you'd already said you didn't want to
spend the night in the emergency department. I might
stab your foot with my heel.'

'That's a risk I'm prepared to take.'

She wondered if his words were intended to be
provocative and Lina was unbearably tempted to take
him up on his offer, but what would be the point?
He'd already kept his distance from her since their
intimacy on the flight and had made it clear that was
the way he wanted it to stay. And deep down she was
sensible enough to know that was the right decision,

even if every pore of her body was desperate to feel his fingers and lips on her again.

But dancing with him would be insane—an exquisite kind of torture to be held in his arms in public. So close and yet not close at all. Their bodies touching and tantalising, reminding her of things she was trying very hard to forget. And wasn't she getting a little tired of the conflicting messages he kept sending out to her? 'I'd rather not,' she said. 'If you wouldn't mind. My feet really are killing me.'

He looked *shocked*. There was no other word for it. As if no woman in her right mind would have turned down such an opportunity and Lina experienced a fleeting feeling of triumph of having asserted herself as they left the crowded ballroom.

But her satisfaction only lasted as long as it took to get in the waiting car, when she suddenly found herself thinking about all the balls Salvatore would go to without her and she got an odd, twisty kind of feeling in her stomach. Did all women feel this powerfully connected to the man they had given their virginity to, she wondered—as if they were joined by some invisible life force?

In the dim light of the limousine she was having to avert her gaze from the sculpted perfection of his profile and suddenly she felt a great rush of unwanted longing.

Stop it, she thought. *Just stop it.*

'So, did you find the evening helpful?'

His question broke into the silence and Lina nodded, pleased to have some respite from the muddle of her emotions. She nodded. 'Very helpful. Siena was really interested in my handbag.'

'Your handbag?'

She held the tasselled velvet bag aloft, although all you could really see was the glitter of the beads and the shimmer of the tassel. 'This. She asked where I'd got it from and I told her I'd made it myself. She wants me to call into her studio tomorrow. Says she might be able to do something for me.'

'Wow,' he said softly. 'That is some result.'

Resisting the desire to bask with pleasure beneath his obvious approval, Lina gave another brief nod. 'Possibly. But I'm not going to build my hopes up until I've spoken to her.'

'Very wise.'

'Yes.' Deliberately, she averted her gaze from him to stare fixedly out of the window as the San Franciscan night flashed past.

Salvatore observed her stiff shoulders and offputting body language as she sat beside him and told himself he should be grateful she was sending out such an offputting subliminal message because, in theory, that should make it easier for him to resist her. But all he could think of was the growing desire which had been plaguing him with infuriating persistence all evening. He'd told himself she was still off-limits. That putting space between them for a while was necessary—for her sake mostly, so she didn't start having unrealistic expectations. And for his own sake, too—to reassure himself that he could take her, or leave her, as he did all women.

But somehow the chic sophistication of her appearance was skewing his thoughts and making him rethink his decision. Because which of them was benefiting by his unasked-for restraint? Not him, certainly—and not her either, he suspected. Suddenly he wanted to peel off that armour-plated dress and feast on the soft flesh beneath. He wanted to see her writhing helplessly in his arms just like she'd done before.

'Lina,' he said softly as she turned her head to look at him. 'Do you have any idea how much I want to kiss you?'

He heard the shuddered intake of her breath. 'I got... I got the distinct impression that was something you definitely *didn't* want,' she managed, as if the words had cost her a lot to say.

And something about her candour made him answer in kind. 'I'm fighting it,' he admitted huskily. 'And it's a battle I seem to be losing right now.'

Her lips parted in silent invitation and he saw them tremble as he reached across to trace their sensual curve with the pad of his thumb. And when he replaced his thumb with the slow brush of his mouth, he could feel the instant jerk of lust—as powerful as if he were a teenager who'd just discovered sex. It was the slowest kiss in the world and it was also the hottest. Before too long she was clawing at his shoulders and he was pushing her back against the seat, his hands all over the rich satin of her gown. He could hear her murmured little moans urging him on and he wanted to touch her bare skin. He wanted to do that so badly. But the dress was stretched tightly across her thighs and what he emphatically did *not* want was an undignified struggle.

'I have no intention of doing it in the car,' he said evenly. 'Even if you didn't happen to be wearing the world's most constricting dress.'

'I *knew* you didn't like it.'

'I don't give a damn about your dress, other than the fact it's in the way. It needs to be removed as quickly as possible and I think that could best be done in the comfort of my bedroom.' He paused. 'Unless you have a better idea?'

He could see the faint doubts which drifted across her face, like the flashes of gold from the passing streetlights. He could banish those doubts by telling her stuff she wanted to hear. Weasel words and soft enticements. Things he didn't mean. Things he could never mean. But he had never made false promises to get a woman in his bed and he never would. Either she accepted him for the man he was, or she got nothing.

She was sitting perfectly still and the intricate confection of her dark hair made her look like a cool and beautiful stranger. 'I can't think of one,' she said, in a whisper.

As the car swung in through the electric gates and security lights illuminated the grounds, Salvatore felt the heavy beat of anticipation. The house was quiet as he took Lina up to his private suite, as he had taken women there many times before, but never had he felt this hungry. He offered her a drink but when she refused he was glad, leading her straight into the bedroom, taking the small velvet bag from her hands and placing it on a nearby chair.

He bent his head, kissed her and began to undress her, sliding down the zip of the fitted dress with a little difficulty until the rich fabric concertinaed to the ground, leaving her wearing underwear which was almost certainly new. Salvatore's eyes narrowed. The delicate bra and matching thong panties undoubtedly made the most of her curves—so why had he started to ache with something which felt like nostalgia for the no-nonsense white knickers he had encountered on the plane?

Very soon she was completely naked and he removed the last of the pins from her hair. And as her black curls tumbled free, he was filled with a rush of lust so pure and so instant that he made a small growling sound beneath his breath.

'You are so beautiful,' he rasped.

'I'm… I'm not.'

'Believe me, you are.' And she was. Because now she looked like Lina again. Like the earthy Sicilian beauty who had given him her innocence. Her firm curves were outlined against his white sheets and her nipples were thrusting little points of deep rose, just begging for his lips to kiss them again. She was bending her knees and her soft fleshy thighs were parting and suddenly Salvatore found himself mesmerised by the dark triangular blur at their apex, as if he'd never seen a naked woman before.

A shimmer of resentment heated his blood as he tore off his own clothes, in between giving her one hard kiss after another, because his hands were shaking like a drunk's and he had drunk nothing stronger than water all evening. But all that resentment had melted away by the time he was straddling her on the bed, watching her awe-struck face as he made that first sweet thrust. And soon after that, he was wondering if he was ever going to be able to stop coming as he bit back a word which was rushing from the very depths of his lungs, a word which might just have been her name.

CHAPTER NINE

It was the most beautiful view she had ever seen.

From the comfort of Salvatore's king-sized bed, Lina stared out at the bright blue of the distant bay. Beneath the fine linen sheets she was completely naked and her cheeks grew warm as she remembered what Salvatore had said just before he'd left for the office at some unspeakable hour this morning, when he had observed her silently watching him from her prone position.

'That was fantastic.' His gaze had met hers in the reflection of the mirror as he knotted his silk tie.

'Yes.' Her voice had faltered and it was only afterwards that she realised how servile she must have sounded. 'Not that I've got anything to compare it with, of course, but I—'

'Believe me, Lina, it *was* amazing,' he had interrupted, almost as if having to make the admission wasn't something he particularly relished. He had glanced down at his watch with the relief of someone lost at sea who had suddenly spotted a lifeboat. 'I really have to go,' he'd said.

His goodbye kiss had been brief, almost perfunctory—as if he couldn't wait to get away from her. As if daylight had destroyed the potent alchemy of what had taken place between them during the night, when her body had felt as if it were on fire every time he'd touched her.

A glance at her phone reminded her she had an appointment with Siena Simon, who'd told her to call by the store at noon. But it wasn't until she had got out of bed that Lina realised her predicament. Her expensive dress lay discarded on the floor—dropped at the exact spot where Salvatore had removed it from her quivering body when they'd returned from the ball. Exquisite lingerie lay scattered alongside the towering pair of shoes she'd been so eager to kick off. She was marooned in Salvatore di Luca's bedroom with nothing suitable to wear back to her little cottage and through a house which would probably be crawling with staff.

She picked up the cobalt evening dress and quickly put it down again. No way could she wear *that* in the brightness of the morning. Distractedly, she looked around, thinking maybe she could borrow something of Salvatore's, and a quick search soon produced a pair of joggers and a faded T-shirt, which carried the name of some band she'd never heard of. The outfit was way too big but at least it was anonymous and Lina rolled up the joggers before quickly gathering together her clothes and tucking them under her arm.

Quietly opening the bedroom door, she cocked her head to listen. The distant hum of the vacuum cleaner sounded a long way off and, judging herself safe, she set off along the corridor, her bare feet making no sound on the bleached wooden floor. She had almost reached the front door when a perfectly modulated English voice almost made her drop her clothes.

'Good morning, Miss Vitale.'

Composing her face into a fixed smile, Lina turned round to see Henry who was wearing a pair of striped grey trousers and what looked like a black tail-coat, and, not for the first time, thought how uncomfortably *hot* it must be if you were a butler.

'Good morning, Henry.'

'Will you be requiring breakfast? Chef has made fresh pastries and kedgeree and...'

He paused, delicately, and despite Lina's total lack of experience at handling this type of situation she somehow knew exactly what he meant.

Did the chef usually provide his boss's lovers with a sumptuous breakfast in one of the two dining rooms, or was it ever served on the terrace?

She gave a weak smile. 'I'm fine, thanks. I'll have something back at the cottage.'

'If you're sure.'

'Quite sure.' She pulled her shoulders back. 'Thank you, Henry.'

'Very good, Miss Vitale.'

Lina made her way through the gardens, where legions of staff were pruning, spraying and mowing various patches of lawn. She could see them turning to watch her as she passed and it struck her how unfair this situation was. You could count on one hand the number of times she'd spent the night with a man, yet this was the second time she'd had to endure a humiliating walk of shame next morning.

But she had nothing to be ashamed of. She might not have Salvatore's social status or wealth, but last night she'd truly felt as if they had come together as equals. He had trembled when he'd touched her. He had moaned almost helplessly as he had entered her. And when, afterwards, she had whispered her lips over his chest to cover it with tiny, tentative kisses— he had given a low rumble of a laugh and tangled his fingers in her curls and told her she was beautiful. And just like last time he'd said it, he had made her *feel* beautiful.

Back in her little cottage, she quickly showered and dressed and fished out the three handmade bags she'd brought with her from Sicily, putting them carefully in a canvas tote. Then she let herself out of the cottage and, with the aid of her cell phone, set off to walk downtown to Siena Simon's store.

She found it with pleasing ease—a large double-fronted building, situated in a pretty tree-lined street. Inside, it was vast and cleverly lit, showcasing some of the designer's iconic designs, all of them worn by impossibly tall and skinny mannequins. Scattered throughout the room on racks and glass shelves of different heights were handmade shoes and exquisite shoals of jewellery. Everything gave off a costly patina and, in her simple cotton dress, Lina felt self-conscious as a beautiful assistant sashayed towards her, a slightly bemused smile on her face—as if doubtful whether Lina was a bona-fide customer. Which, of course, she wasn't.

'May I help you?'

'I hope so. I'm looking for Siena Simon.'

The assistant's smile became even more doubtful. 'Do you have an appointment?'

'Well, I met her at a ball last night and she—'

'It's okay, Tiffany.' The drawled words were followed by the appearance of a figure at the back of the store, and suddenly there was Siena Simon dressed in her trademark cream, with a pair of gravity-defying shoes and a choker of pearls at her throat as big as gulls' eggs. 'I asked Nicolina to call by today,' she said, and then smiled. 'Good to see you again, Nicolina. Did you bring any more of your work with you?'

Rather self-consciously, Lina held up the canvas bag containing her totes. 'They're all in here.'

'Good. Why don't you come on through to my office and I'll have Allegra fix us some coffee?'

Lina nodded. 'Sure.'

The interview which followed was daunting and yet, in a funny kind of way, it was also one of the most rewarding things which had ever happened to her, and when Lina emerged just under an hour later, it was with a feeling of excitement bubbling away inside her. She'd almost dropped to the floor when Siena had informed her just how much she could charge for one of Lina's little handbags and had instantly agreed to make as many of them as possible. She had a job—of sorts. Wasn't this the first step on the road to independence?

She wondered what to do next, whether to find herself a sandwich for lunch, or try to hunt down a second-hand sewing machine. She had just decided that the latter option would be the most sensible, when she noticed a tall and powerful man who was walking purposefully along the street.

In her direction.

He was instantly recognisable on so many levels—visual, visceral and emotional. Lina's heart squeezed as her eyes feasted themselves on the blue-black gleam of his hair and the coiled strength of his muscular physique. She had been trying not to think about him all morning. Trying to concentrate on work and ambition and thoughts of the future and wondering what an independent life would look like. But now that she'd seen him, all those thoughts seemed to crumble away because that was the effect of the strange power he had over her. Lina felt her stomach dissolve as he reached her and for a moment or two it felt as if she'd forgotten how to speak.

'Salvatore.' She licked her lips like a starving cat which had just spotted food. 'This…this is a surprise.'

'I came to meet you.'

'But you didn't know where I'd be.'

'Obviously, I did, otherwise I wouldn't be here.' His blue gaze mocked her. 'You told me you were going for an interview with Siena—remember?'

Of course she remembered, she was just surprised he had—because hadn't he seemed more concerned with plunging into her body for the umpteenth time, rather than hearing about her plans for the following day? She looked at him in confusion. 'But I still don't understand why you're here.'

Salvatore wasn't quite sure about that himself—and felt a flicker of irritation that she'd been gauche enough to draw his attention to it. Because hadn't the voice of reason warned him against coming here, telling himself to leave it until the end of the day, at least. Telling himself that a few hours' grace would give him time to untangle himself from the potency of the spell she seemed to have cast over him. And then he'd thought: what the hell? He wanted to have sex with her again and as soon as possible—and judging by the smoky darkening of her eyes, she was feeling it too. 'I thought we could have lunch.'

'Lunch?'

'There's no need to make it sound as if I've made an indecent suggestion. Though I'm perfectly prepared to do that afterwards,' he murmured. 'And you're really going to need to stop blushing like that, Lina.'

'I can't help it,' she whispered. 'And I haven't got time for lunch. I have to get hold of a sewing machine.'

'You can do that later,' he said firmly. 'Just get in the car.'

At last it seemed to dawn on her that he wasn't taking no for an answer, but her stumbling reluctance was surprisingly charming, and as he lifted his hand to summon his car, he could feel lust spearing through him like a hard and relentless arrow. And just as soon as the vehicle moved away, he pulled her into his arms and started to kiss her, her squirming excitement turning him on even more.

He had intended the kiss to be hard and swift—

a possessive declaration of his intention to seduce her as soon as they'd eaten. But instead it became a deep and drugging interaction which dragged him down into some dark and silken place, and maybe her hungry response had a lot to do with that. As she curled her fingers around his neck and pressed her breasts against him, his passion for her combusted. His heart was pounding as he realised they had approximately twelve minutes until they reached the restaurant. Time enough for what he wanted. He could slip his hand beneath the hem of her sundress and quickly bring her to a shuddering orgasm before unzipping himself so that she could take him in her mouth as she had done so exquisitely last night. He could tell the driver to keep circling the block until he tapped on the window. It wouldn't be the first time he had done it.

But somehow, with Lina, it didn't seem *appropriate*—and although it was the most difficult thing he'd ever had to resist, he drew away from her and tersely instructed her to smooth down her ruffled hair. As the car drew up near the Embarcadero, he found himself perplexed by his own behaviour, but reassured himself that the wait would be worth it—and a demonstration of his rigid control would not go amiss.

The restaurant was crowded and Lina's predictable delight on her first sight of the iconic bridge view was pleasing, though she seemed oblivious to the fact that people were turning their heads To look at her, despite the many society beauties who were dotted around the place. Would it have surprised her to know that her naturalness was like a breath of fresh air in the rarefied atmosphere of this famous city eatery? he wondered.

Soon they were seated at his usual table, with crisp linen, crystal and silver laid out before them, as waiters and sommeliers clustered around them. Salvatore ordered lobster and salad, a bottle of cold water and a dish of olives, before leaning back in his chair to study her.

'It sounds like your interview with Siena went well,' he observed.

'I think so.' She hesitated as she picked up her napkin and shook it out. 'She asked me lots of questions. How well I knew you. How long I was planning on staying in the city. That sort of thing.'

'I guess she wants to be sure you'll stick around if she's planning on giving you work.'

'I guess.' She hesitated. 'She seemed particularly interested in the fact that I was living with you.'

He frowned. 'But you made it clear that we're not actually living together?'

'Of course I did,' she said, and hesitated again. 'It just made me wonder...'

His gaze bored into her. 'What did it make you wonder, Lina?'

She had started pleating the edge of her napkin now, as if unable to keep her fingers still.

'If you'd ever been in a relationship with her.'

'No. I've never been in a relationship with Siena,' he said slowly. 'Would it bother you if I had?'

Abruptly, she stopped pleating and looked up. 'It's nothing to do with me who you've had a relationship with.'

'So you wouldn't mind if I brought a woman back to the house?'

'Of course I wouldn't.'

'Liar,' he said softly.

Lina stared at him, shaking out her napkin in an attempt to remove the pleats. She had been finding the whole situation daunting, even before he'd said that. The fancy restaurant with a terrifying amount of cutlery. The other diners, who were watching them while pretending not to—or, rather, watching *him*. The realisation that once again they had slept together last night and indulged in all kinds of delicious intimacies. And now he had accused her of lying. 'Excuse me?'

'It *would* bother you, Lina. It's bothering you right now just to think about it—it's written all over your face. But that's okay. It's perfectly normal to feel sexual jealousy in a situation like ours.'

She told herself to leave it. That his use of the word 'ours' was not meant to be inclusive and it certainly wasn't meant to give her hope—and bearing in mind how arrogant he could be, she was amazed that she even *wanted* to be hopeful where Salvatore di Luca was concerned. But wasn't it funny how all the reasoning in the world didn't stop you yearning for something you knew was ultimately futile, so that you came out and asked the question anyway? 'And what exactly is our…situation?'

'Difficult to define,' he said, his blue gaze splintering through her. 'I wasn't intending for us to continue to be lovers once you came to America. I thought it was better if our relationship became platonic since you were going to be living on my property, but that clearly hasn't been the case.'

Lina told herself to leave this one, too. To maybe change the subject and ask him about that woman on the far side of the restaurant who was clearly trying to catch his eye. But the newly liberated Nicolina Vitale wasn't intending to spend the rest of her life being a moral coward by avoiding subjects which had the potential to be tricky, was she? Hadn't she done that too often in the past, with her mother? Played safe to keep the peace—and look where that had got her.

Last night in bed, she had felt like Salvatore's equal—and wouldn't someone who was truly equal refuse to be a coward and ask the difficult questions, questions that previously she wouldn't dare ask, just in case she didn't like the answers? She lifted her water glass and took a sip from it. 'Why?'

He said nothing more until the waiter had placed the food in front of them and, although he gestured for her to help herself, Lina didn't move.

'I think we both know the answer to that. Because it's pretty obvious to me, at least, that I can't seem to resist you, despite all my best intentions.'

'Okay…' she said uncertainly, wondering why his words sounded more like an insult than a compliment.

'But you're worlds away from my usual kind of partner, Lina.'

Lina had been about to help herself to a portion of avocado, but now she put the serving spoon down, strangely repulsed by the sight of all that glistening green flesh. 'And what's your usual kind of partner?'

He picked out every word with forensic care. 'Women who know the score. Who understand the way I operate.' His blue eyes darkened, like sudden storm clouds appearing on a summer's day. 'And if we are to continue like this as lovers, you need to know the score too. I can offer you fidelity and generosity for as long as we're together, but commitment is a non-starter. So if you think this is going to end with a golden band gleaming on your finger, then it's over as of now.'

It took Lina a moment to realise what he meant. 'And you think all women want to marry you—is that what you're trying to say?'

'In my experience, yes.'

Lina shook her head because his poise was breath-taking, as was his cool arrogance—unless he was simply telling her the facts as he saw them. But maybe it didn't matter what motivated his words, she either agreed to his terms, or he walked. He would and could do that, she realised. Despite all the push-me, pull-me stuff he'd been doing these past few days—if he thought she was getting serious, she wouldn't see him for dust. Even if he missed the sex, it wouldn't be for long. You only had to look at the expressions of some of the women in this restaurant to know that here was a man who was universally lusted after. He would soon replace her with some-one else, someone who was more his 'type'.

And Lina wasn't ready to let that happen. Not yet. She wasn't ready to turn her back on this incredible awakening, because of some kind of misguided idea that deeper emotions had to be involved. You didn't have to be in love to do what they were doing. Those kinds of beliefs belonged in storybooks, or within the repressed confines of the tiny village into which she had been born. Hadn't she come to America to shake off those old-fashioned assumptions?

'Well, I don't want to marry you,' she said, making sure she kept her voice very quiet in case someone overheard and thought he was actually *proposing* to her. 'That's not the reason I'm here. I told you back in Sicily that I had dreams and they haven't gone away. And Siena has shown me that I might be able to make those dreams a reality. I'm never going to conquer the world, I'm sensible enough to realise that, but if I can make a decent living for myself, then I'll be satisfied.'

She could see the sudden hard burn of his eyes. The sudden tightening of his lips. 'I'm glad we understand each other, Lina,' he said softly, casting a rueful glance down at the untouched food in front of them, before lifting his charged blue gaze to her. 'And since you've brought up the subject of satisfaction, let's take it one step further. It doesn't look as if either of us are going to do this meal justice—so what do you say we get out of here so that we can spend the rest of the afternoon in bed?'

Lina's heart was thumping as she stared back at him across the table. He had suggested going back to have sex as coolly as if he were calling for the bill, and part of her wanted to do that, despite the callous things he'd said. Because now she knew something about his background, didn't that make his cynicism more understandable? He'd been lied to and deserted at an impressionable age by his mother—the one person he should have been able to rely on above all others. Why *wouldn't* he develop an aversion to close relationships after an experience like that? Then he had grown spectacularly successful and perhaps been targeted as much for his wealth as his rugged beauty, though she would have desired him just as much if he'd been a poor fisherman, like his father. And wasn't there a part of her which wished he were? That he came unencumbered, without all the homes and staff and fancy aeroplanes.

But Salvatore wasn't looking for understanding or compassion. His needs were simply physical and Lina needed to cultivate a similar mindset if she wanted this to continue. And she did. Why let her own emotional vulnerability spoil her very first sexual relationship?

But even so…

He needed to understand that from now on she wouldn't be a pushover. That he couldn't just click his fingers to have Lina Vitale fall in with his plans. That he needed to respect her as well as desire her.

'Tempting,' she said. 'But I can't really afford the time right now.'

She saw his look of surprise.

'You're kidding?'

Lina shook her head. 'I told you, I have a sewing machine to buy and materials I need to order so that I can make my handbags. I promised Siena I'd have three prototypes with her as soon as possible so I need to get on with that.' Her smile was serene but maybe that was because her words were making her feel positively *empowered*. 'And since you know the city better than I do, perhaps you could take me shopping?'

CHAPTER TEN

A RED LIGHT on Salvatore's desk was flashing and the disembodied voice of his assistant echoed around the vast office.

'Miss Vitale on three, Salvatore. Are you in, or out?'

It was a question his assistant had asked him many times in the past when a woman had called, and his answer would inevitably provide some clue about the state of whatever relationship he happened to be in. During those early days of heady sex, he was usually indulgent if a lover rang him at the office, although he never encouraged it. A couple of weeks in and he was prepared to be tolerant, but by the one-month mark he was inevitably irritated if he was disturbed—because by that stage there seemed little to say to a woman which couldn't wait until later.

Yet with Lina it seemed to be different. It had been different from the start—and all the times in between. Like that surreal afternoon when she'd turned down the opportunity to go to bed with him—and had him accompanying her to bizarre fabric wholesalers, in areas of the city he hadn't even realised *existed*.

And she had been true to her word about working hard. Each day she spent working in her little cottage before emerging blinking into the light like a little animal which had been underground, her eyes tired from sewing but with a look of immense satisfaction on her face as she sewed handbag after handbag.

Her hand-crafted wares had been snapped up by Siena Simon and, after a little questioning on his part—for Lina was nothing if not modest—he'd discovered they were creating something of a buzz, not just in San Francisco, but beyond.

Salvatore had been quietly impressed with her endeavours, for there had only ever been one other woman he'd shared a living space with before Lina, and she couldn't have been more different from his idle, entitled mother.

He was just perplexed that he seemed content spending more time with her than was usual with a woman. Was it because she was living on his property that he found himself unable to keep her at his preferred emotional distance? Or because she spoke to him exclusively in Sicilian dialect—a language which nobody else in his orbit understood? Their shared tongue locked them both in a private world which sometimes felt achingly familiar, yet, at others, darkly claustrophobic. He had expected to be bored with her by now. For the allure of the simple country girl to have become tarnished by exposure to the bright lights of the city, but to his surprise—though it hadn't been a particularly welcome one—that hadn't happened.

And his thoughts were growing increasingly troubled.

Because hadn't he become faintly *obsessed* with the Sicilian dressmaker? Hadn't he found himself endlessly fascinated by the way she slowly brushed those waist-length black curls, knowing he was watching her? Her eyes would sometimes meet his with the faintest hint of mockery lurking in their bourbon depths, as if in silent acknowledgement of his vehement demand that she never wear her hair up again.

Hadn't he broken the rule of a lifetime and taken her to every damned tourist destination in town, watching almost indulgently while she cooed her way through each tour with breathless delight? And hadn't her genuine enjoyment of San Francisco's famous sights made him view his adopted city with a different, less cynical eye? Yet most of all, he relished those intimate moments when they were alone together and he could observe her soft wonder as he pleasured her. She never shut her eyes when he was inside her. That smoky bourbon gaze was always fixed unwavering on his. Sometimes the intimacy of that made him uncomfortable—sometimes not. All he knew was that her voluptuous body pleased him immensely, as did her generous nature. She never used sex as a weapon, or a bargaining tool as had happened in the past. In fact, she never asked him for anything. There had been no 'casual' references to diamonds or pearls. She hadn't even hinted that she might like to use one of his cars. For a man who was forever being tapped for money, this was a first.

But Salvatore was discovering disturbing parallels between himself and his father. Because his father had been obsessed with his wife, hadn't he? He'd let his hunger for her rule his life. And that had been his downfall. It had taken Salvatore a long time to realise why his mother had been so cruel to her husband, in a way which had impacted so negatively on all their lives. It had taken adulthood and his restless flight to America before he was able to work it out for himself, through his own relationships. Only then was he able to understand the inevitable power struggle which existed between a man and a woman, and how finely balanced it was. He'd discovered that some women despised men who loved too much and craved the ones who did not love at all. He'd had that demonstrated over and over again. His emotional indifference seemed to have inspired slavish adoration from the opposite sex. Or perhaps he was simply seen as a challenge. As a prize to be won.

Men who loved made themselves vulnerable, he realised.

And he was never going to be vulnerable again.

Wasn't it time he proved that—not just to Lina, but to himself?

'Salvatore?' His assistant's voice broke into his reverie. 'Are you still there? Do you want me to put Miss Vitale through, or shall I tell her you're in a meeting?'

Salvatore's mouth tightened. And wasn't it *insane* how disloyal it felt—to contemplate colluding with his assistant to tell a blatant untruth to Lina? She had never rung him at the office before, had she? What if she was in some kind of trouble—what if she needed his help? 'Put her through,' he gritted out.

'Salvatore?' Lina came on the line and just the way she said his name was like having cool water sprinkled on a heated brow.

'Is something wrong?' he demanded.

'No, nothing's wrong.'

Relief gave way to desire and he could feel it coursing through his veins, but infinitely more disturbing was the sudden race of his heart in response to her soft voice. 'Then why are you calling me at the office?' he growled. 'I'm working.'

'Yes. I know that.'

He could hear the sudden insecurity which edged her words but forced himself not to react to it. Because she needed to know that this kind of behaviour was a sure-fire way to hasten the end of their relationship, and he wasn't quite ready for it to end. Not yet. 'What can I do for you, Lina?'

'I just wondered what time you would be home.'

It was the most mundane of questions and it filled Salvatore with a cold dread because it embodied the kind of cloying domesticity he had spent his life avoiding. 'You called me to ask me that?' he questioned, not bothering to hide the faint incredulity in his voice. 'I'll be home before seven, same as always. Why do you need to know?'

'It doesn't matter,' she answered hurriedly. 'I'll see you later.'

Lina replaced the telephone with nervous fingers as she tried to block out Salvatore's terse response to her question, wondering why he had gone so cold on her. Maybe she shouldn't have rung him at the office, but surely it was okay just this once—when she was preparing a surprise for him. And she *wanted* to surprise him, as well as celebrate her own good news. To give something back. Because hadn't he been incredibly generous towards her? Hadn't he taken her in against his better judgement and given her a roof over her head, thus allowing her to find her feet? Yes, she had promised to pay him back—and she would—but that was going to take time.

She began to crack eggs into the flour and to mix them together, the rhythmical movement reminding her of a thousand pasta dishes she'd made back home. But these days she felt completely different from the woman who had endured that miserable existence. At first she hadn't been able to believe that life could be like this—that every day could feel special—and she knew much of that was down to Salvatore. It had been hard to get her head around the fact that someone could make you feel funny and sexy and desirable, without even really trying.

Sometimes he would turn up at her cottage if he finished work early, looking utterly irresistible in his suit, his immaculate appearance marred only by the loosening of his tie, which had the effect of making him appear rakish. And even though she would remind him that they weren't supposed to be seeing each other until later, she would invite him in, as casually as if he were paying nothing more than a social call, just in case one of his staff happened to be passing. But the moment the door had closed behind him, she would be pushed up against the wall while he kissed her as if he were trying to suck all the breath out of her lungs and she'd be tearing at his clothes like a wild thing. Sometimes they didn't even make it as far as the bed. It was electric between them. It always had been—he'd told her that more than once. Lina could feel the sudden rush of warmth to her cheeks and wondered if every woman felt like this in the early stages of a relationship. As if you'd discovered a new kind of power, but, weirdly, as if you'd lost a different kind of power in the process.

Because lately it hadn't been all roses and moonlight and she'd been plagued by doubts, which she couldn't seem to push away, no matter how hard she tried. Nagging doubts which lurked in the shadows of her mind, just waiting to spring on you when you least expected them. She'd started wondering if she had allowed herself to become a victim of her own self-deception.

She'd thought…

What?

That she could neatly compartmentalise her life, so none of the edges would overlap? That she could sew all day and deliver her little handbags to Siena's store, where later they would appear on the arm of a mannequin, or on one of the tables or glass shelves, all at an eye-wateringly marked-up price? That she could do all this and try to pretend the other stuff wasn't happening. The stuff which felt real but which wasn't real. Stuff which involved Salvatore. Because, somewhere along the way—during all the meals and the tourist trips and the sex-filled nights—something had changed. Her fixed ideas had shifted and altered and the subject of sex didn't seem so black and white any more. She knew all about the whole friends-with-benefits thing because Salvatore had painstakingly explained it to her. She'd thought she understood it. She had signed up for it knowing it was all he was prepared to offer and convinced herself she was okay with it. She'd thought she could handle it.

But suddenly she was having difficulty handling it because something had changed. In her, not him. Not suddenly and not overnight. It had been like the drip, drip, drip of a leaking tap which somehow managed to fill an entire bath before you realised it. At first she'd thought it was because of the sex. That the response he drew from her eager body was the reason for the erratic see-sawing of her mood. But the dreamy aftermath of yet another shuddering orgasm didn't explain away the yearning in her heart as she bit back the tender words she was longing to say to him. She wanted to run her fingers through his hair and whisper her lips across his mouth at the most inappropriate of times. She felt as if she was falling in love with him.

Her fingers dug into the pasta dough. These were just complicated feelings for a man who didn't want emotion—the trouble was that she wasn't sure how to deal with them. Because she didn't *want* to feel this way. She wanted to wake up one morning and be free of all this aching and yearning deep in her heart. Yet instinct warned her that wasn't going to happen. The same instinct which knew the relationship would eventually run out of steam, unless she had the courage to push it in a different direction.

Was it a flicker of her newfound confidence at work which made her willing to give it a try? Her handbags were proving surprisingly popular and had been flying out of the store. It seemed that rich women were prepared to pay a lot of money to own something so obviously handmade. Siena Simon had become a big fan of her work, prompting her to talk to the features editor of one of the biggest fashion bibles in the country, which had produced an exciting result. Which was part of the reason for this meal. But only part of it. Lina felt her chest tighten with apprehension. Because she wanted to give Salvatore something which all his billions couldn't give him. She ran her fingertips over the gleaming purple flesh of the aubergine. Some heart. Some thought. Some care. Something which had been made from… not love, no, because that would freak him out. But surely it was okay to demonstrate her deep affection and her gratitude to him, by cooking him a simple meal.

Her preparation finished, she stole a quick glance in the kitchen mirror at the hair which she'd tied back so it wouldn't flop in the sauce. A smile curved her lips as she touched her fingertips to an imprisoned wave. Better unpin it before Salvatore got home…

At first he couldn't find her. In fact, he couldn't find anyone. The house was unusually silent and there was no sign of Henry, or Shirley, who often served dinner.

Salvatore flared his nostrils, like an animal finding itself in unknown territory which had begun silently sniffing the terrain for threats. There had been a faint foggy drizzle in the air tonight and the table had been set for dinner in the smaller of the two dining rooms, rather than out on the terrace. Tall lit candles flickered a golden light show across the creamy walls and the air was thick with the scent of cut roses. Almost automatically he noticed crystal glasses and a bottle of champagne chilling in a silver ice bucket and a feeling of disquiet whispered down his spine. Just then Lina came running up from the kitchen, her cheeks pink with exertion, a scarlet dress clinging to her abundant curves and her luscious curls bouncing around her shoulders. Usually, he liked her in red, but tonight his senses were on alert and he wasn't quite sure why.

'What's going on?' he questioned. 'Where is everybody?'

'It's Henry's night off and I told him we didn't

need any replacement help.' She smiled. 'And I gave the chef the night off.'

He stared at her. 'You did what?'

'I didn't think you'd mind. He works very hard and seemed very pleased to have an unexpected free evening. I've cooked you something myself instead.' Her smile became a little uncertain. 'We don't need anyone else.'

'That is beside the point,' he said impatiently. 'Since when did you start taking over roles which were never supposed to be yours, Lina? Or did you think that several weeks of sharing my bed has given you carte blanche to exert your will and start dismissing my staff whenever you saw fit?'

'No! Of course I didn't.'

'Then why didn't you run it past me first?'

'Because…because it was supposed to be a surprise.'

Ever since the day when he'd arrived home from school to discover his mother ready to drive away with that slimy salesman, Salvatore had had an abiding contempt for surprises. But from the dark hurt he could see clouding her eyes, he wasn't going to tell her that, in case she switched to unwanted sympathy. The last thing he would be able to stomach would be her compassionate tears on top of everything else. 'Fine,' he said, forcing a quick smile. 'Why don't you just serve it up?'

He could see from her pinched expression that she was feeling wounded and, while that didn't make him feel particularly good, he was unwilling to repent. Because hadn't he been soft around her? Too soft, maybe. Had he been blinding himself to the truth because it had suited him to do so? Intoxicated by her vibrantly passionate nature and their unique sexual chemistry, he had ignored the very obvious signs that she was starting to care for him. He plucked the champagne bottle from the bucket and began to tear off the foil. And that was the last thing he wanted.

He had just poured out two glasses when she carried the steaming dish into the dining room and Salvatore felt his stomach heave as he detected the familiar smell. 'What's this?' he asked, even though he knew damned well what it was.

'Pasta alla Norma,' she said, just a little too brightly. 'Your favourite.'

But it didn't feel like his favourite right then. It felt as if two very different worlds had just come crashing together, leaving him disorientated by the fall-out. Ignoring the generous portion she served him, he slanted a questioning glance at the glass of champagne which he handed to her. 'Are we supposed to be celebrating something?'

She sat down opposite him and he realised he hadn't even kissed her and somehow that seemed very relevant, because this was the first time he had ever looked at her without desire. And she was the one who was killing it, he thought furiously. Destroying a perfectly good relationship with high-handed behaviour and her manipulative attempts to rein him in with an unwanted domesticity which felt like the doors of a jail clanging closed.

'It's *kind* of a celebration,' she said, with a smile.

He forced himself to go through the motions of appearing interested although his mood was so dark, all he could manage was a single word. 'Oh?'

'The good news is that my bags are selling well and the store is very pleased—more than pleased. In fact, it's as much as I can do to keep up with demand and Siena has spoken to a features editor at *Trend* magazine.'

'A features editor at *Trend* magazine?' he repeated blankly.

She nodded, and her thick black hair shimmered in the candlelight. 'It's the number one fashion bible and they want to do a piece for their accessories issue. And Siena thinks we should have a party at the end of the month, to make the most of all the publicity. Open some champagne and invite some of the city's movers and shakers, that kind of thing.'

'How is advertising your wares going to help if you're already struggling to keep up with demand?' He took a sip of wine. 'Talk me through that one.'

'Siena thought we might be able to employ out-workers. You know, women who can't do regular hours because they have young children. It means…' She gave an almost embarrassed shrug of her shoulders. 'It means we could increase production and widen our reach.'

'And make you a household name in the process, I suppose?'

Her voice sounded defensive. 'That was never my ambition, Salvatore.'

'But it looks like it might happen anyway.' He pushed away his plate and lifted his champagne glass in a toast. 'Congratulations. I guess that means you'll be able to start looking for a place of your own very soon.'

It hurt.

Lina bit her lip. It hurt way more than it should have done, mainly because she hadn't been expecting it. It was a curve ball, as they said over here. Lina had been busy cooking a surprise meal and buying a bottle of champagne because she wanted to share her good news with him. And he just wanted her out of here.

Well, of course he did. That had been one of the conditions for letting her live here in the first place. That she would be here for a few weeks and no more. What had she expected? That wall-to-wall sex would have made him start reconsidering his initial intention that she leave, and he'd tell her she could carry on living in the cottage for as long as she liked? *In your dreams, Lina. In your dreams.*

'You've barely touched your dinner,' she observed.

'I could say the same about you.'

'I thought you liked it.' She pressed her lips together. 'You ate it on that beach in Sicily as if it were going to be your last ever meal. I can remember it as if it were yesterday.'

He shrugged, lifting his hands in a silent gesture of apology. 'I guess it's like buying a shirt when you're in a foreign country—it never looks quite the same when you wear it at home, does it?'

'No. I guess not.' Lina felt deflated as she cleared away the dishes and carried them down into the kitchen and she was standing over the sink when she sensed, rather than heard, Salvatore enter the room behind her. She could feel the sudden, subtle change in the atmosphere. The way it became charged with electricity—like the heavy, thick thrum of air you got just before a thunderstorm.

For once he didn't tease her about her opposition to dishwashers as he sometimes did if he caught her washing up coffee cups in her little cottage. Did he guess she didn't want to meet his probing gaze right then, that she was terrified he would read something of her emotional turmoil in her eyes? Did he realise how stupid she felt because somewhere along the way she had fallen for him, despite all his warnings to the contrary? Was that why he walked across the room and wrapped one hand around her waist, using the other to lift up a heavy curtain of hair so he could kiss the back of her neck, his lips brushing lightly against her skin. And wasn't it infuriating that she could feel a whisper of response shivering its way down her spine, despite the discord of the meal they hadn't shared?

'Did I mention that I have to fly to Rio de Janeiro first thing tomorrow morning?' he murmured into her hair.

'No, you didn't tell me.' She dunked a saucepan into the hot, soapy water and tried not to react to that seeking kiss. 'How long will you be gone?'

'A couple of weeks.'

'Right.' She tried to stop her breathing from become ragged even though all she could think was that they'd never been parted for that long before and, more crucially, he was only announcing it now—at the last minute. Do you think you'll be back in time for the party?' she asked calmly.

'I'll do my best.'

It was not the answer she'd wanted but it seemed it was the only one she was going to get. She closed her eyes and wondered what he would do next.

She wanted him to leave.

She wanted him to stay.

He turned her around and started to kiss her and, to her shame, she let him. No, that wasn't strictly accurate. There was no shame involved in any of this—only pleasure. She was giving as good as she got and kissing him back with a fervour which felt angry as well as hungry. And maybe those two words were easier to muddle up than she'd initially thought. It felt as if she wanted to punish him. Which she did. As if she wanted to hurt him as much as he had just hurt her. It might have been wrong but it felt so right and he laughed softly against her lips, as if he were trying to provoke her into an even more passionate response. And he was getting one, because now it was rapidly getting out of control. Her hands flew to his shoulders as he bent her back towards the table and his teeth were grazing at her breasts though the thin jersey of the red dress. Her nipples puckered into painful points as he rucked up her dress and she heard his ragged murmur of desire. She felt so wet and she could hear the rasp of his zip as roughly he freed himself, followed closely by the sound of crashing china and cutlery as he swept it off the table and it hit the kitchen floor.

But Lina didn't care and she didn't stop. She didn't think anything could have stopped her right then, she wanted him so much. He ripped off her panties, damp, tattered fabric fluttering down to join the other debris, to the accompaniment of her own slurred words of approval. She was barely aware of him tearing open a condom and putting it on before opening her thighs and positioning himself. He thrust right up to the hilt and never had he felt bigger or harder or more aroused. She came so quickly it took her by surprise—though not him—for he gave a moan of relieved satisfaction as he followed her, his jerking body taking a long time to subside afterwards.

He buried his head in her curls, which were spread like a black cloth over the table, and when she turned her head to survey the shattered glass and crockery, she could see the pasta already congealing, like tomato-covered snakes. She had wondered if he might show remorse or regret, but there were neither as he brushed his mouth over hers in a careless kiss, before slowly following the direction of her gaze.

'To hell with domesticity,' he grated. 'There's only one thing I want to see you doing in my kitchen, Lina, and it's this.'

CHAPTER ELEVEN

THE DECORATED STORE looked as if Christmas had arrived early and there was barely an inch to move. Lina hovered near the entrance, busy scanning the new arrivals who were being waved through by security guards, and trying not to look as if she was waiting for someone—which of course she was. She gave a quick glance at her watch. Where *was* he? She could see Siena walking towards her—her cream chiffon evening dress floating behind her like a cloud—and she smiled at the designer who had been so kind to her.

'What are you doing hanging around by the entrance instead of out there basking in the glow of your success?' Siena questioned.

Lina's smile didn't slip. She'd been producing it at regular intervals since the party had kicked off with a blast of Sicilian music, cascades of twinkling rainbow lights and non-stop pink champagne. No need to tell Siena that she was waiting for Salvatore and didn't have a clue what time he was getting here. That he hadn't called her since the day before yesterday, saying that the line was bad and his schedule busy. Or that there had been several long, awkward silences throughout a conversation he clearly hadn't wanted to have. Was that why they had talked about the weather, and how long the flight had taken and whether the famous Brazilian feijoada dish was as delicious as everyone said it was. Because ever since that night when they'd had sex on the kitchen table, it had felt as if there were more than just the gulf of a different country between them. And she couldn't quite shake off the dark ache of foreboding, for she suspected things were ending between them.

She looked at the designer, who was twisting a long rope of pearls around her finger. 'I was just looking out for Salvatore's car.' Lina shrugged. 'Because I'm guessing people will want to see him.'

'Oh, people always like to see Salvatore di Luca.' Siena slanted her a wide smile. 'But you're the star here tonight, Lina, and don't you ever forget that. You can be perfectly successful in your own right, with or without your billionaire lover.'

Lina wondered if that was simply a kindly intervention from the older woman, warning her not to rely on a man who was only ever going to be a temporary fixture in her life, but she nodded, even if right then she didn't really believe it. 'Thank you.'

'You are going to speak to the journalist, aren't you?' Siena continued. 'He says he's a little worried. He thinks you've been avoiding him all evening.'

'But... I've already given an interview to *Trend* magazine.'

'Yes. I realise that.' Siena twirled her pearls round and round her forefinger. 'But the local paper has a very popular gossip column, which is bread and butter for people in the luxury-brand business. It shouldn't be too onerous. Just tell him a bit about yourself. How you got started and what you like doing in your spare time. Readers love that kind of thing.'

A sudden lump sprang up in her throat and Lina swallowed because this was the bit she was terrified about. What could she possibly say to elaborate on the basic facts of her life—that she enjoyed sewing little beads and sequins onto squashy pieces of velvet and making each one different? That she enjoyed pottering around in Salvatore's huge gardens whenever she got the chance and felt a distinct sense of achievement that she had finally managed to get the frosty Henry to warm to her a little. But her main passion was for Salvatore, and that was the trickiest part of all.

Because her feelings for him had grown in a way

she'd never planned. Maybe that was why the power balance between them had shifted so radically that she now felt as if they were living in different dimensions. And it had all happened since she'd cooked him that wretched meal. Since she'd stupidly tried to take their relationship onto another level.

Nervously, she swallowed. 'Must I?'

'It's essential,' said Siena firmly. 'In fact, here's Brett Forrester now and he's heading our way. Look, why don't you take him over there, away from the music deck—go and stand over by the evening coats, where it's quieter?'

Lina's heart was racing as she watched the journalist making his way towards them. Brett Forrester was a man in his late forties with a ridiculously over-long blond fringe flapping into his eyes, which she thought might have looked better on someone two decades younger. Ditto his leather jacket and very tight jeans. Shunning the champagne, he seemed welded to a tumbler of whisky, from which he constantly sipped, and he gave Lina a critical once-over as Siena introduced them before diplomatically drifting away in her cloud of chiffon. The greetings over, he raised his arm and a woman with an enormous camera instantly appeared by his side.

'We'll get some shots of you now, and a few more when your boyfriend arrives,' he said, his voice very slightly slurred.

A flash exploded in Lina's face, and she blinked in alarm.

'I don't think—'

'Lick your lips, honey. Stop looking so scared. Camera's not going to bite you—and don't forget this is all for *your* benefit.'

Was it? Lina wondered why this whole evening was suddenly starting to feel as if she'd released a monster from a cage. She hadn't realised just how many people would be attending, or that they'd be crammed into the huge space of Siena's store like sardines in a tin. The music was too loud and the half-glass of pink champagne she'd drunk was already giving her a headache. In fact, the only friendly face she'd seen all evening had been Sean MacCormack—the soap actor she'd sat next to at the charity gala when she'd first arrived in the city, and Salvatore had insisted on buying her that designer dress, which she hadn't worn since. But she had worn it tonight because it was the only thing in her wardrobe which was halfway suitable and, despite Salvatore's preferences, she had worn her hair up—mainly to showcase some of the jewellery which the store also stocked. Which is why she currently had two waterfall diamond earrings dangling by the sides of her neck, along with a matching bracelet which flashed rainbows whenever she moved her wrist.

At least tonight's party had proved an effective

distraction, barely giving her time to think, let alone brood about how bad it had been between her and Salvatore before he'd flown to Rio. Awful didn't come close to the way that night had ended. She had insisted on clearing up the mess they'd created on the kitchen floor and had insisted he help her. At first he hadn't believed she meant it—as if someone like him shouldn't have to participate in something as ordinary as housework. But she had held firm, her emotions still running high after the furious words they had shared and the highly charged sex which had followed.

'Do you think it's magically going to clean itself?' she had demanded. 'Or that one of your staff should have to deal with it in the morning? You were the one who threw everything on the floor!'

'I didn't hear you objecting at the time!' he had flared back.

He had been angry and moody and she had felt... *weird.* As if he'd used her, even though she'd enjoyed every second of it and had been an active participant. She'd figured out that the best thing to do would have been to have taken herself off to her cottage and spent the night apart from him. To have given them both the space she'd suspected they needed to cool down.

But something had held her back from walking away from him. Maybe it was because sometimes, in the darkness of the night, she felt closer to him than at any other time. Not necessarily during sex, but afterwards, when he would lie stroking her hair, his voice lazy and reflective. As if within the enclosed space of their bedroom none of the worries and cares of the outside world existed. As if, for a few brief moments, he allowed all the barriers with which he surrounded himself to crumble to the ground.

And that was why she had allowed him to take her in his arms and kiss her again, once they'd finished scrubbing at the kitchen tiles. Because in the face of all her growing insecurity about the future, his embrace had felt comforting and safe. And that was just an illusion, she reminded herself bitterly.

And then she looked up and saw Salvatore standing on the other side of the crowded room, his eyes trained unwaveringly on her, and everything else just faded away. Lina's heart burned, as if someone had punched a red-hot fist to the middle of her chest. She'd told herself she was going to get over him and prove she didn't need him—emotionally *or* physically. But what power on earth could ever make her immune to him?

Salvatore felt a stab of awareness as his eyes connected with Lina's and a wave of something extraordinary flowed through his body like a powerful surge of electricity—an effect she had on him which no other woman had ever been able to match. Two whole weeks had passed yet it seemed he was still susceptible to her particular magic. But she could make him angry as well as filling him with desire, and he was angry now, because he didn't want to feel this way.

Not about her.

Not about anyone.

His gaze scanned over her and he realised she was wearing exactly the same outfit as the night he'd taken her to the gala ball, when he hadn't recognised her. But tonight he wasn't having any difficulty recognising her, despite the rigid gown and intricately coiled hair. Because no amount of face paint or gilding could deflect from a sensual and earthy beauty which needed no artifice. His eyes narrowed as he noticed the man beside her—some creep of a journalist he thought he recognised. And as the man moved closer, Salvatore experienced a savage jolt of something which felt like possessiveness. His throat dried. Or was it protectiveness?

He began to walk towards them and flinched as a flash went off in his face, but he carried on walking, weaving his way through the crowd and ignoring the sound of people vying for his attention and the hopeful smiles of so many women, until eventually he reached Lina. The man with the ridiculous hairstyle brightened and held out a hand, which Salvatore ignored.

'Hi! Brett Forrester of *San Fran Daily*. We've met before. At the races last year. Do you remember?'

'No, I don't,' said Salvatore repressively, but the other man failed to take the hint and leave.

'So, what do you think about your girlfriend's designs, Sal?'

Salvatore felt his fists tighten as the nickname he never used took him right back to the schoolyard. Suddenly, he had the urge to lash out, in a way he hadn't wanted to do since those circling fights when the other kids had taunted him and called his mother *puttana*. Did Lina guess at his discomfiture—was that why she put her hand on his bunched forearm, her fingers acting as the gentlest of restraints, just as the blue-white flash of a camera exploded around them?

'We don't have to stay, you know,' she said, very quietly, blinking against the bright light. 'We can leave any time you want.'

He resented her understanding tone. He wanted to tell her that he didn't *need* her kindness or her soft compassion. That he could manage perfectly well on his own. 'But this is your night, Lina,' he answered dangerously. 'Surely you want to enjoy every second of your success?'

Did the journalist sense the sudden scent of conflict in the air? Was that why he pulled out a notebook and a pencil? 'Tell me how you two met.'

Salvatore's gaze was stony. 'That is not for public consumption.

Still the journalist didn't give up. 'But you're both Sicilian, yes?'

'Listen to me,' said Salvatore in a voice of silken finality. 'The evening has obviously been an absolute triumph for Miss Vitale, though in future it might be better if you gave your subject matter a little more personal space. And that's the only quote you're going to get from me, Forrester. Understand?'

'But—'

'The *only* quote,' affirmed Salvatore grimly.

Maybe it was the ripple of danger in his voice which finally convinced the journalist to retreat, leaving Salvatore alone with Lina and the furious beat of his heart. She was looking at him nervously, as if she couldn't quite gauge his mood. And the crazy thing was, neither could he. It was as if he didn't dare open his mouth for fear of what was going to come out of it next.

'I'm glad you managed to make it,' she said, her voice edged with a kind of desperation as if she was trying to pretend nothing was happening.

What *was* happening? he wondered as a waiter came by with a tray of drinks and he took a crystal beaker of fizzy water to slake his thirst before looking around the room. 'This is some party,' he observed softly.

'I'm glad you like it.'

'I didn't say that.'

'You mean you don't?'

'I didn't say that, either.' He gave his empty glass to another waiter. 'But doing seedy interviews with journalists like Brett Forrester has never really been my scene.'

Her teeth were chewing on the gleam of her lips. 'Nor mine.'

'Neither do I enjoy the way I was ambushed by the paparazzi from the moment I arrived.'

She looked at him acidly. 'Then maybe you should have surrounded yourself with security!'

He glared at her. 'Maybe I should!'

Her voice dipped into an angry whisper. 'Why did you bother coming at all, when you're in such a filthy mood?'

'I suppose I wanted to support you.'

'Forgive me for saying so, Salvatore, but this doesn't feel remotely like support.'

He knew that. He knew it, but he couldn't seem to stop himself from the bitter words which were tumbling out from somewhere deep and dark within him. Because something bitter had begun to harden inside him. Something which was making it difficult for him to breathe. He looked around to where one of Siena's assistants was standing in front of a queue of people, tapping out frantically on her tablet—presumably compiling a wait-list.

'You've come a long way from the woman who just wanted to make a living,' he observed softly. 'You've changed, Lina.'

She was shaking her head as if she couldn't quite believe what he was saying. 'Of *course* I've changed,' she whispered. 'I had to. Didn't *you* change when you came here? Didn't you feel you had to do that, so that you'd blend in? Or do you think I would have fitted into this glitzy city if I'd just bombed around on my little bike, wearing dusty old sneakers and frumpy clothes? Maybe that's what you would have preferred me to do?' she added, into the charged silence which seemed to have enveloped them. 'To have stayed exactly the same as I was.'

He stared at the tight shiny spirals of black hair which were coiled on top of her head. At the heavy satin gown which effectively ironed out every one of her luscious curves. At the diamonds which dazzled at her neck and her wrist, their blue-white fire almost as bright as the photographer's flash.

'Yes,' he ground out. 'That's what I would have preferred. Because you don't look like Lina any more.'

'And yet when I *did* look like Lina and behave like her—doing that very traditional thing of cooking a Sicilian meal for you as a surprise—that wasn't right

either, was it?' she questioned. 'In fact, you acted as
if I had committed a terrible crime.'

'Because I didn't sign up for domesticity!' he re-
torted. 'I didn't want some West Coast recreation of
a life I left behind a long time ago!'

She stared at him for a long moment. 'Do you
want to know something?' she said, at last, her voice
low and trembling. 'That I had stupidly started to
care for you? Yes, I admit it—even though you had
warned me against doing so—I had fallen into the
same trap as so many others! I cared because I liked
the man you were underneath all the trappings. In
fact, sometimes I found myself wishing you didn't
have all that damned money, because it suits you
to think women are only interested in your wealth,
doesn't it? Just like I wish your mother hadn't deserted you and your father hadn't neglected you afterwards. But we can't rewrite history, Salvatore, no
matter how much we'd like to. And you will never
heal from the wounds of your past—because you'll
never allow yourself to!'

'That's enough,' he snarled.

'No. No, it's not enough. I've listened to you often
enough when you laid down all your *terms*. The least
now you can do is to hear *me* out. Because no woman
is ever going to be right for you, are they? There is
no female on earth who could possibly fulfil your

exacting and contradictory demands—because they are unachievable!'

'Too right, they are. And do you want to know why?' He stabbed his fingers into the air, in a way she'd seen him do once before. 'Because I don't want all that *stuff*! I don't want domesticity and living by the clock. And I don't want children, either—do you understand? Children who become the unwilling victims of the mess their parents make of their relationships! I'm not seeking the chains which other men strive to anchor themselves with. So why don't you do yourself a favour, Lina—and stay away from me?'

Lina's throat was so dry she could hardly breathe and the fitted dress felt as tight as a shroud. She would have run out of there—she *wanted* to run out of there—but she couldn't. Not with these stupidly high heels and a wall of people in front of her. But importantly, she knew she *shouldn't* run away, even if it were physically possible. Not with her potential future lying in front of her. Here there were potential clients and potential backers and she couldn't just storm out of there because her heart felt as if it were breaking. Siena had taken a chance on her and given her the opportunity of a lifetime and now her efforts were finally beginning to bear fruit. And this had been what she'd wanted, hadn't it? In fact, her ambition had over-vaulted itself and not only had she achieved far more than she would ever have believed possible, but Siena had told her that a lot more lay ahead.

More than that, she had learned something about herself along the way. In her eagerness to please people and keep the peace, Lina had allowed herself to ignore the way they were treating her. She had pretty much always fallen in with other people's demands. Her mother had done it and now it seemed she was in danger of letting Salvatore do it, too. He wasn't interested in what she wanted—only in his own closed and selfish agenda.

And suddenly, she could feel her nerves and her fears slipping away from her. Somehow she would get through the rest of the evening and the rest of her life, just not with Salvatore. Never again with him. Why try to cling to a man who could be so hurtful? Why chase after something he would never be prepared to give her? Because she had wanted this. Worked hard for it. Was she really going to let it slip away because she was pursuing someone who had always been beyond her reach? She owed herself more than that.

So, although her heart was beating so hard that it hurt, she tilted her chin and fixed him with a cool look. 'Look, you're clearly not enjoying yourself and I really ought to circulate. So why don't you go on ahead? It looks like I'm going to be here for some time.'

He shook his head. 'I'll wait,' he said.

'No.' Her voice was quiet, but determined. In fact, she'd never felt quite so determined in her life. 'Honestly. Just go. I really don't need you here.'

He opened his mouth as if to object, as if her sudden poise had perplexed him. As if he were the only one in this doomed relationship who was allowed to make decisions. But what could he possibly object to, when she was giving him everything he wanted?

He'd provided her with an escape route, hadn't he? Surely now she could return the favour.

CHAPTER TWELVE

SALVATORE STARED AT the newspaper which had been placed neatly on his desk and the anger which had been smouldering inside him since he'd got out of bed that morning now threatened to combust. Splashed all over the inside pages was a feature about last night's launch party for Lina's handbags, with the usual shots of seasoned attendees presenting their best sides to the camera, their posed smiles in place. But it was the photograph of him with Lina which disturbed him most, the one with her hand on his arm, which had inspired the excruciating headline speculating on whether San Francisco's most famous bachelor had finally lost his heart to a woman from his homeland. Which made a pulse begin to flicker at his temple.

If he looked closely—which he seemed to be doing, despite his initial inclination to crush the of-fending journal in his fist—then he could see something in her unguarded expression which disturbed him. Which seemed to vindicate his determination to move on from her. He swallowed. For wasn't her Madonna-like face soft as she looked at him, her dark eyes full of the care she'd confessed she felt for him? He felt his heart clench with something which felt like pain, but instantly he blocked it out. Because he didn't do that kind of pain. Not any more.

Pushing the paper away, he looked up at his assistant who had appeared at the door, carrying a tiny cup of super-strong espresso, her sharp attention immediately drawn to the article in front of him.

'You've seen it?' she said. 'I thought it best to draw your attention to it. I know you never usually read that rag.'

He took the coffee from her and sipped. Delicious. 'Must have been a slow news day,' he said acidly. 'Could you bring me in the files about the orphanage in Romania, please, Maggie? As quickly as possible.'

He could tell from her slightly aggrieved expression that she was irritated by his terse response and lack of additional information, but Salvatore didn't care. He didn't want to discuss it any more. Not with anyone. The subject was closed. He disposed of the newspaper and threw himself into his work, and for several hours it proved engaging enough to allow him to forget all the domestic trivia which had been weighting him down of late. He told himself he should be celebrating what looked like the end of his liaison with Lina, and the freedom that would bring. But the crazy thing was that several times he found himself wanting to lift the phone and talk to her. He frowned. He didn't usually ring her from the office. But then, he was usually sated from a blissful night of sex, which kept him going until he saw her again at dinner time. With narrowed eyes he gazed out of his office window, but for once he failed to be dazzled by the spectacular view across the rooftops to where blue sky met blue water.

Because there had been no sex last night, had there? Irritated by her cool assertion that she would prefer to remain at the party without him, Salvatore had indeed jumped into his waiting limousine and been driven home. But he hadn't gone straight to bed. He had sat out on the softly lit terrace, with music playing in the background, looking up at the stars. On a purely logical level he had been aware that the relationship was approaching its final meltdown stage and would soon be over. But it hadn't quite reached that stage and he hadn't stopped wanting her, just as he knew, deep down, she hadn't stopped wanting him. So why shouldn't they both capitalise on that? They had entered this arrangement sensibly, which meant there was no reason why it shouldn't end on a similar, sensible note.

He had been feeling almost nostalgic as he'd

waited for her and the minutes had ticked slowly by. He might open a good bottle of champagne and they would toast her success before retiring to his bedroom and satisfying each other in a way he'd been missing ever since he'd flown to Rio. And who was to say that some kind of arrangement like that couldn't continue, once she had moved into a place of her own?

He heard the sound of the electric gates opening and a car stopping. The slam of a door, and her softly accented voice saying goodnight. His body tensed as he waited for her.

But Lina didn't come.

She must have known he was there, for the drift of the music would have reached the courtyard and she would have looked up to see the lights on.

Why didn't she come?

Slow minutes ticked by before it dawned on him that she must have gone straight to bed and his initial surprise and faint outrage was replaced by the quick stir of desire. He was tempted to go over to her cottage and let himself in, as he'd done so many times before. To steal inside and take her silently, absolving them both of the need to talk about what had happened tonight. He wanted nothing more than to lose himself in her soft body. To press his lips against her silky, cushioned flesh. He wanted to feel her tense when he was deep inside her and then to shudder with mindless pleasure. Because wasn't that the one thing which was always right between them, no matter what else was going on? But he was damned if he was going to tacitly admit he'd done something *wrong*, following her like a chastened puppy which wanted to be forgiven.

He'd wondered if she might appear this morning to share a coffee with him before he left for the office as she sometimes did, but she hadn't done that either. And that was when his anger had begun to ferment into an ugly brew. No matter what was happening between *them*—something which had always been on the cards—shouldn't she at least have shown a little gratitude that he'd turned up at the damned party and given it his seal of approval?

He left work early and rang for some iced water as soon as he got home, but Henry didn't answer his summons immediately, and when he did, he looked so unlike his usual unflappable self that Salvatore was forced to ask:

'Is something wrong?'

'It's Miss Vitale, sir. She's gone.'

'What do you mean, she's *gone*?'

But Henry shook his head, almost as if he were *upset*, and Salvatore got up immediately and went straight over to the cottage, surprised by what he found there. Because she really *had* gone. Bedlinen had obviously been laundered and neatly piled up on the mattress and every small room had been scrubbed clean. There was no trace of her. No clothes or books. No sewing machine or velvet. No beads—other than a couple of tiny droplets which were glittering on a rug and which she must have missed when she'd been vacuuming.

Confused now, Salvatore reached into his jacket pocket for his cell phone—and that was when he saw the fat-looking envelope, propped up on the mantelpiece next to a small jam jar of flowers she obviously couldn't bear to throw away. He ripped it open and withdrew a sheet of writing paper and, mystifyingly, a large wedge of dollars. It was the first time he'd ever seen her writing, he realised—and it was curving and easy to read. A bit like her, he thought with a pang, before allowing righteous anger to flood through him as he read her words.

Dear Salvatore,

It's difficult to know how to start this letter, but I guess first of all I must thank you for bringing me to America and giving me a home until I was able to establish myself.

It has been a roller coaster of a ride and it looks as if my dream to make something of myself has exceeded anything I could have ever thought possible.

I've moved in with Sean for the time being.

Sean? Salvatore thought, with a frown. Who the hell was Sean? His eyes scanned the letter again and he could almost hear her soft voice answering his question.

> *Do you remember? He's the lovely actor I sat next to when we went to the gala ball.*
>
> *He's got an apartment in Haight Ashbury and says I can have a room there for as long as I need it. So that's what I'm going to do.*
>
> *Please could you forward any letters from my mother?*
>
> *You'll find some money in the envelope, which covers the cost of the dress and the shoes you bought me for the gala ball. Please accept it, with my thanks.*
>
> *If starting this letter was difficult, I'm finding it even harder to end it. Maybe I'd just better say that I will never forget you, Salvatore, and that I wish you every happiness.*
>
> *Yours, Lina.*

How ironic, he thought, his body tensing. Over the years he'd received texts and cards liberally adorned with kisses, from women who meant nothing to him. And yet not a single *x* followed Lina Vitale's name.

How could something like that hurt?

How could he *let* it hurt?

His cell phone was ringing and he snatched it out of his pocket, a faint feeling of disappointment washing over him when he saw it was Maximo Diaz, even though he was a good friend from way back. He was tempted to ignore the call, but why ruffle the feathers of one of the most powerful men in Spain, and one with a notoriously tight schedule?

He clicked on the 'accept' button. 'Maximo?'

'Usually, my phone calls are accepted with a little more enthusiasm that that, my friend,' mocked the rich voice of the wealthy industrialist.

Salvatore gave a short laugh. 'Forgive me. It has been a long week. Good to hear from you, Max. What can I do for you?'

'I'm coming to San Francisco at the end of the month. I thought that maybe we could catch up. Unless you're too occupied with this woman I've seen you pictured with in the papers.'

Salvatore's mouth hardened. 'Absolutely not,' he said firmly. 'That ship has sailed and I'd love to spend a night on the town with you, like the old days.'

Why not? he thought as he terminated the call. They were both virile and eligible men.

And they were both single.

His jaw tightening, Salvatore put the phone back down on his desk.

* * *

Haight Ashbury was certainly *buzzy*.

Sean's apartment was directly above a Chinese restaurant—which offered them a discount on its delectable food. To Lina's surprise there was a beautiful tree planted on the pavement outside—along with numerous stalls selling rainbow flags and badges, and music by people she'd never heard of. It was a bit strange to get used to jostling tourists taking photos of the iconic building whenever she went outside, but Lina convinced herself it made good sense to have such a startling change of circumstance.

Because this is my new life, she told herself fiercely.

With Sean's help she pushed her bed up against the wall, creating as much space as possible for her sewing machine, her velvet and beads. Her actor flatmate's hours were long. He started early, didn't get back until late, then spent much of the evening learning his next day's lines. It certainly disabused Lina of the idea that an actor's life was one of glamour.

He'd asked her questions, of course. Or rather, he'd tried. But she had explained very firmly that she didn't want to talk about Salvatore. She didn't feel ready to and her emotions were still so volatile that she was terrified of bursting into tears.

Anyway, it was over. Salvatore hadn't bothered ringing after she'd left him that letter, or tried to get in touch. She'd told herself she hadn't been expecting him to and had tried very hard to crush her aching disappointment. What had come as a bit of a surprise— a gut-twisting shock, if she was being honest—was when, yesterday morning, Sean had shown her a picture taken of Salvatore and some darkly-handsome man, emerging from a famous San Franciscan nightclub. Lina had stared down at the photo with a feeling of growing dismay, because behind the two men it was possible to glimpse the tanned and toned legs of two gorgeous blonde women. The twist in her gut had tightened. That hadn't taken him long, had it? Less than a month and it appeared he was dating again.

She had spent a miserable night after seeing that, waking up this morning bad-tempered, with a headache and craving a sugar rush, which was why she'd gone down to the nearby bakery to buy herself some breakfast. She was just offloading her frangipane croissant onto a plate in Sean's cluttered kitchen, when she heard the sound of the doorbell.

It was probably a delivery, Lina thought as she ran down the rickety wooden staircase to answer it. Sean seemed to spend his life ordering things online, then sending them back again.

It wasn't.

Standing on the doorstep, and somehow managing to own every bit of the space around him, was Salvatore. In his immaculate suit, snowy shirt and silk tie, he looked very formal against the colourful backdrop of Haight. But then she noticed his unshaven jaw and the dark shadows beneath his tired eyes and a very instinctive spiral of jealousy made her want to slam the door in his face.

But that wouldn't be dignified. It would be tantamount to showing him she cared—and why on earth would she do that?

Instead, she injected her voice with friendly enthusiasm, as if they were old friends who'd just met again after a long absence. 'Salvatore, this is a surprise! Did you bring my mail?'

'Your mail?' he repeated blankly.

'From my mother. You remember? I said I was expecting a letter. You could have forwarded it, you know.'

'There is no mail.'

'Oh. Right. She's obviously still sulking. She has ignored every letter and email I've sent her.'

'I didn't come here to talk about your mother.'

'Oh?'

He was glowering at her now. 'Aren't you going to invite me in, Lina?'

There was a pause. 'I wasn't intending to, no.' He appeared to be waiting for an answer and so she gave him one, even though every pore of her body objected to sending him away. 'I can't see the point,' she said in a low voice. 'There's really nothing left to say, is there?'

Salvatore felt the painful punch of his heart as he looked at his soft Madonna and noted the unusually stubborn set of her chin. He thought how incredible she looked in that short cotton dress, her thick hair dangling over one shoulder, and he thought how unbelievably stupid he'd been. He felt a jolt of rage and pain which stirred somewhere deep inside him. 'Can we please go inside?' he said. 'Because I don't want to have this conversation on the doorstep.'

There was a split second of a pause when he actually thought she was going to refuse him entry, before she gave an ungracious nod. 'You'd better come in.'

'Thanks.' Quickly, he stepped inside and shut the door before she could change her mind, following her up a scratched wooden staircase and into a small, untidy kitchen. A take-away cup of coffee was cooling on the side, next to a sickly-looking croissant.

'Are you hungry?' she asked.

'No. But please don't let me stop you eating breakfast.'

'I'm not hungry either. Not any more. Look, why don't you just tell me why you're here, and then let me get on with my work?'

Salvatore had spent the whole night and all the journey here working out exactly what he planned to say, but suddenly his breath caught in his throat as a dark wave of fear washed over him. A fear like nothing he'd ever felt before, and he had only himself to blame. Because what if it was already too late? What if he'd blown it with his arrogance and his control-freakery and his inability to really let go of the past?

That was a chance he had to take. A chance all men took when they put their feelings on the line. When they met a woman they were willing to take a risk for, and when they'd behaved like a fool. But even so…this was pretty scary stuff. 'I've been a fool, Lina,' he said, and looked at her.

'You won't hear me denying it,' she said.

Had he thought that would be enough? That she'd open her arms and forgive him with the minimum of fuss? Yes. He had. But it was not enough, he could see that now. He sucked in a deep breath and tried to continue but it wasn't easy to express himself. Hell, he'd never *had* to express himself like this before. 'You made me look at the past and realise that I was in danger of ruining the rest of my life if I wasn't careful.'

'I'm pleased for you,' she said primly.

Did she want *more*? It seemed she did. 'The house feels empty without you and so does my bed. I miss your soft smile and your laugh and the way you sometimes lose your temper,' he said and then, when she didn't speak, he sucked in another breath and said the words very carefully, just to make sure there could be no mistake. 'The thing is, that I love you, Lina Vitale. I didn't want to. I didn't plan to, but I do.'

If he had been expecting laughter, or tears, or gratitude, he got none of those. Just a faintly hostile expression which radiated from the depths of her bourbon eyes.

'Did you say that to one of the women you were with last night?' she asked, in a voice he'd never heard her use before.

'What women? Oh!' He clapped the flat of his hand against his brow. 'You're talking about the women outside the nightclub?'

She gave a bitter laugh. 'You mean there are more?'

'None. None at all. They spent the night following us round the club like detectives and were as devious as a pair of foxes—we only managed to shake them off once our car had arrived. Listen to me, Lina. Hear me out—that's all I ask.' His throat felt as if someone had attacked it with a blowtorch but somehow he managed to fire the words out. 'I've spent the past few weeks telling myself I'm no good for you, that you'd be better off without me, and, yes,' he admitted, 'that I'd be better off without you.'

She was silent for a moment, then turned and

stared out of the window, as if she'd rather look at a mosaic of Jimi Hendrix than at him.

'Go on,' she said, in a small voice.

'An old friend of mine flew into town yesterday and we decided to…'

'To what, Salvatore?' she quizzed, whirling round to face him as his words tailed off. 'What did you decide?'

He sighed. He'd wanted to go to the nightclub to see what effect it had on him. He'd hoped to find an easy solution to his ongoing heartache in the form of one of the women who regularly swarmed over him. He'd thought he might be able to forget about Lina and the way she made him feel. But he couldn't forget. What was more, he didn't want to. The glitzy women who had tried to come onto him had meant nothing. They never had done. Only this woman had got close to him, despite him doing his level best to push her away. And that was when he'd realised how hard he'd tried to protect himself from emotional pain. That, for all his towering success, he could rightly be accused of being a coward. That with his charitable work he had attempted to help people who'd been deserted and never known love— he had just neglected to help himself in the process.

'I decided I needed to come and tell you the truth,' he bit out. 'Which is breathtakingly simple. That I love you. You and only you.'

'Salvatore,' she said, a little desperately, and now her face had become a twisting conflict of emotions, so that for a minute it looked as if she was about to cry. 'Don't say any more.'

'I have to. Listen to me, Lina. Please.' His plea was heartfelt and maybe she guessed that, for she grew silent again. 'I fell for you the first time I saw you, in a way I'd never done before. It's why I broke the rule of a lifetime and had a one-night stand. You blew me away with your freshness and sweet charm and made me feel as if you wanted me for the man I really was. But it suited me to disregard that simple fact, because you also made me feel like I was losing control, and that was the one thing I had relied on in my life, in order to survive.' He paused. 'The only thing.'

'That was why one minute you pushed me away and the next, you were pulling me back again,' she said slowly. 'Why you kept saying about how you liked me to look. That's why you liked to dictate how I wore my hair.'

'It's true I prefer it down,' he admitted.

'To be honest, so do I.'

He swallowed. 'I thought that if I could control you, then...'

'Then you would have all the power and I would never leave you the way your mother left you. You didn't want anyone to be able to hurt you like that ever again.'

His throat was tight and he could hardly breathe, because her level of understanding was devastating. It was as if she knew what he was thinking. As if she could peer deep into his soul. But whereas once that thought would have filled him with dread, now it filled him with awe.

'But I've come to realise that by playing safe,' he continued bitterly, 'I am closing myself off to the greatest potential for happiness I've ever known. Because when you weren't around I discovered how empty my life felt. And I realised that by trying to control you, I risked crushing your inner strength and that burgeoning independence which makes me love you even more. And that is why I'm asking you to forgive me, Lina. Forgive me and stay with me and let me make amends. I want to marry you, if you'll have me, so I can spend the rest of my life loving you, as you deserve to be loved.'

She didn't have to think about it for long, because Lina knew there could only be one answer to a question she hadn't dared ever believe he'd ask. She had admired him from afar and then she had loved him up close. She'd seen the darkness in his soul and had wanted to flood it with daylight. She didn't care about his money. If he told her he wanted to go and live in Caltarina in a little house like the one she'd grown up in, she would be happy with that. Then she thought about her mother living down the road and thought…well, maybe a different village.

She opened her mouth to tell him all these things, but she was so overcome with emotion that the words just wouldn't come. And perhaps he read her answer in her eyes, because his own were suspiciously bright as he pulled her into his arms and kissed her. It was a long time after that kiss had ended, and the coffee on the kitchen counter had grown completely cold, that she brushed her finger along the shadowed edge of his unshaven jaw. 'You know, I'll never hurt you, Salvatore.'

He dipped his head to capture her fingertip and nipped at it with his teeth. 'You can't say that.'

'Yes,' she contradicted, more certain now. 'I can. Oh, sometimes we might fight, or disagree—because that is the way of the world. But my heart is so full of love for you, that there's no room for anything else and there never will be.'

His eyes grew hard, and bright. She saw in them understanding, and fear. But the fear would fade in time. Love would make sure of that. It would soothe and smooth everything in its path. It would comfort and reassure. And it would also provoke—in ways which were emotional as well as physical.

She shivered as he stroked his thumb over one peaking nipple.

'I think it's time for bed,' he said, a little unsteadily. 'Don't you?'

EPILOGUE

'READY?' QUESTIONED SALVATORE.

Lina looked up into the glitter of her husband's beloved blue eyes and nodded. 'Ready,' she said.

The limousine was waiting outside to take them to the airfield. Soon they would be high over the skies of California, en route to Caltarina—their first trip since they'd married there, last year.

It had been the most gorgeous wedding Lina could have imagined—an unfussy ceremony, the tiny church bursting to the rafters with a mix of villagers and many of Salvatore's jet-setting friends. Siena had been there, eying up some Greek tycoon, and Lina had insisted on Henry, Shirley and Salvatore's chef, Ric, being present. There had been huge excitement when Sheikh Kadir Al Marara had flown in for the reception, and Lina's mother had been in her element, boasting to anyone who would listen that her beloved daughter was marrying one of the richest and best connected men in the world. But Lina didn't let that bother her—to be honest, she was so happy that nothing could bother her.

Reconciled soon after the announcement of her engagement, and determined to forget the harsh words of the past, Lina had asked her mother to make her wedding dress, and throughout those fittings they had talked in a way they'd never done before. Each stitch sewed into the delicate organza seemed to have helped heal their fractured relationship. She had learnt of her mother's desperate loneliness after the death of her husband and her realisation that she had transferred all that pain onto her daughter. Yet Lina's departure for the United States had forced her mother to re-evaluate her life, and to forge a new way of living, which was bringing her an unexpected kind of contentment.

The wedding dress had turned out to be a triumph of simplicity and Lina had worn her hair loose— of course. A single photograph of the happy couple had been sold to news outlets around the world, with all the profits going into Salvatore's charitable foundation.

A foundation for which Lina now worked, alongside her husband, because she'd decided that dispossessed children were closer to her heart than accessories for the rich and privileged. But she hadn't given up completely on her unique designs.

Her handbags were now made by a dedicated team of out-workers and there was huge competition for these jobs, because the rates of pay were so favourable. There had already been talk of diversification. Of shawls and evening shoes, with the looping Lina signature embroidered on every product. There was also a simple Lina scent—an evocative lemon fragrance meant to evoke images of sunny Sicilian days.

She was happy about her success and the fact that all profits went into the foundation. But most of all Lina was happy because Salvatore loved her with all his heart. He told her so every day, and every day she echoed that sentiment.

But…

She looked up to find him watching her, his eyes narrowed with interest. He was so intuitive, she thought happily.

But…

Her heart was beating very fast and she knew she couldn't put it off any longer. 'How…how would you feel about us having children?'

Salvatore didn't answer straight away, but then, he was pretty sure she didn't expect him to, because this was way too important not to give it his full consideration. But he didn't have to think about it for very long.

'I want to have a baby with you,' he answered simply.

Tears sprang to her eyes. 'You're sure?'

He nodded. 'As sure as when I knew I wanted to spend the rest of my life with you. But this isn't an academic discussion we're having here, is it, Lina?'

'I don't know how it happened!' she burst out.

He was smiling. 'You don't?'

'That's not what I mean. I don't want you to think that I—'

'Shh.' He pulled her into his arms and he could feel the pounding of her heart against the race of his own as he buried his lips in her hair. 'Contraception hasn't been my number one focus lately. It just seemed less important. I've probably been careless.' He smiled against her thick black curls. 'Or just too damned relaxed.'

She drew back and searched his face, dazzled by the blaze of his blue, blue eyes. 'You're saying…?'

'I'm saying that it feels right,' he said huskily. 'Just like you feel right. You always did.'

'And you think… You think we'll be okay parents? You're not scared?'

'Of course I'm scared,' he admitted slowly, in a way he would never have done to anyone else. But Lina had made him realise that it was okay to express your doubts and fears, and that being strong didn't mean you couldn't also be vulnerable. He cleared his throat. 'But we know what we do want for our baby,' he husked. 'And, more importantly, what we don't want. And we've got each other, Lina. We can help each other along the way.'

'I love you, Salvatore di Luca. Do you know that? I love you so very much.'

Her face was wet as they kissed and when he drew back and wiped her tears away, he shot a calculating glance at his watch. 'I think we could allow the car to wait a little longer.' His hands on her shoulders, he looked deep into her eyes. 'Don't you?'

'That depends,' she said, a little breathlessly. 'On what you had in mind.'

'You know exactly what I have in mind. I want you. And I want you right now.' The words came out ragged. Emotional and deliberate. It was a statement he'd made many times before but with Lina it meant something different. It meant way more than sex.

It was all about love.

* * * * *

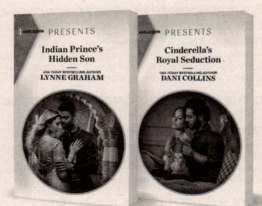

COMING NEXT MONTH FROM

⊞HARLEQUIN
PRESENTS

Available March 17, 2020

#3801 THE INNOCENT'S FORGOTTEN WEDDING
Passion in Paradise
by Lynne Graham

After a terrible car crash, Brooke can't remember her own name—much less her wedding day! So finding billionaire Lorenzo at her bedside—and a gold band on her finger—is completely shocking...

#3802 THE ITALIAN'S PREGNANT CINDERELLA
Passion in Paradise
by Caitlin Crews

Billionaire Cristiano can't get the unexpectedly innocent Julienne out of his head. He's sure another night together will cure him... until her bombshell destroys his fiercely controlled life! Because his onetime Cinderella is carrying the next Cassara heir...

#3803 KIDNAPPED FOR HIS ROYAL HEIR
Passion in Paradise
by Maya Blake

Determined to claim his child, Zak demands pregnant Violet meet him at the altar. And when she refuses? This powerful prince will keep Violet a willing captive on his private Caribbean island until she says, "I do!"

#3804 HIS GREEK WEDDING NIGHT DEBT
Passion in Paradise
by Michelle Smart

Theo has one goal: seeking vengeance on his runaway bride! Yet Theo can't escape their past...or the intense connection that spectacularly reignites. Will this tycoon be tempted to rewrite the rules of his revenge?

HPCNMRA0320

#3805 THE SPANIARD'S SURPRISE LOVE-CHILD
Passion in Paradise
by Kim Lawrence
Softhearted Gwen had always dreamed of the day tycoon Rio
would discover their child. Yet the reality is astounding! Because
when the brooding Spaniard sweeps back into her life, he
demands their daughter—and her!

#3806 MY SHOCKING MONTE CARLO CONFESSION
Passion in Paradise
by Heidi Rice
He's Monaco racing royalty and I, Belle Simpson, was his
housekeeper. But that evening, Alexi's searing gaze exhilarated
me. Five years later, I finally have the chance to reveal my secret—
Alexi's a father!

#3807 A BRIDE FIT FOR A PRINCE?
Passion in Paradise
by Susan Stephens
Samia's thrilled by the longing Prince Luca awakens within her
but knows a temporary fling is their only option. A future with him
is impossible. For the shadows of her past make Samia wholly
unsuitable...don't they?

#3808 A SCANDAL MADE IN LONDON
Passion in Paradise
by Lucy King
Kate is *mortified* when billionaire Theo discovers her secret dating
profile. Yet she can't resist his tantalizing offer to introduce her to
pleasure beyond her wildest imagination! But the biggest scandal
of all is yet to happen...

_____

**YOU CAN FIND MORE INFORMATION ON UPCOMING HARLEQUIN TITLES,
FREE EXCERPTS AND MORE AT HARLEQUIN.COM.**

HPCNMRB0320

*Theo has one goal: vengeance on his runaway bride,
Helena! But Theo can't escape the past...or the intense
connection that spectacularly reignites between them. Will
this tycoon be tempted to rewrite the rules of his revenge?*

*Read on for a sneak preview of
Michelle Smart's next story for Harlequin Presents*
His Greek Wedding Night Debt

Did she realize that every time she spoke to him, she tilted toward him? Did she realize that she fidgeted her way through every conversation? Was she aware that her breath hitched whenever he walked past her? Was she aware that at that very moment her hands trembled?

"The next thing I wanted to discuss is the kitchen," she said, moving the conversation on.

"What about it?" he asked lightly.

She tugged at the sheets of paper he'd placed his backside on. "You're sitting on my notes."

"My apologies." Sliding smoothly off the desk, he went and sat on the chair on the other side of her desk. "Is this better?" But she didn't respond. Her eyes were on his, wide and stark, her fidgety body suddenly frozen. "Helena?"

She blinked at the mention of her name and quickly looked down at her freed notes.

"Yes. The kitchen." Despite Helena's best efforts, her voice sounded all wrong.

It had been hard enough to breathe with Theo propped on her desk beside her—when he'd first perched himself there, she'd feared her heart would explode out of her chest—but when he'd moved off, she'd had to fist her hands to stop them from grabbing hold of him. Now he was sitting opposite her and she'd caught a sudden glimpse of his golden chest beneath the collar of his polo shirt, and in the breath of a moment her insides had turned to mush.

It shouldn't be like this, she thought despairingly. She'd spent three months under Theo's intoxicating spell, riding the roller coaster of her life.

He'd had the ability to make her forget everything that mattered. Under his spell she'd believed all she needed was Theo in her life to be happy. She was sure her mother had once believed the same thing before she'd sold her soul to a monster. Theo wasn't a monster like Helena's father, but his power over Helena had been just as strong.

How could she still react so strongly to him? She'd believed the sudden detonation of their relationship had killed her feelings for him, but she saw now that she'd been hiding them, hiding them so deep inside that she'd forgotten how powerful they were until one look at him in the Staffords boardroom had seen them poke their heads out from dormancy. Now the old feelings were slapping her in the face, taunting her, and it was getting harder and harder to fight them.

Eyes now determinedly fixed on the papers on her desk, she rubbed the nape of her neck, cleared her throat and tried again. "We need to discuss the kitchen's layout. Do you still want to consult a professional chef about it?"

She knew the moment she said it that she'd made a mistake.

Something sparked in his eyes. He leaned forward a little, a satisfied smile spreading over his face. "You do remember."

"Only that neither of us can cook." She quickly fixed her gaze back on her notes, aware her face was flaming with color.

"But you asked—specifically—if I still wanted to consult a chef about the kitchen… What else do you remember?"

She tucked her hair behind her ear and wrote something nonsensical on her notepad. "Have you a chef in mind to consult?"

"Answer my question."

Her hand was shaking too much to write anything else.

"Helena."

"What?" Helena intended for her one-syllable question to come out as a challenge. She might have succeeded if her voice hadn't cracked.

"Look at me," he commanded.

Heart thrashing wildly, she breathed deeply before slowly raising her face. "What?"

His voice dropped to a murmur. "What do you remember?"

Trapped in his stare, she found herself unable to lie. "Everything."

Don't miss
His Greek Wedding Night Debt
available April 2020 wherever
Harlequin Presents books and ebooks are sold.

Harlequin.com

2679

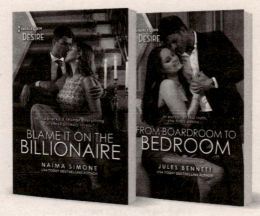

Love Harlequin romance?

DISCOVER.

Be the first to find out about promotions,
news and exclusive content!

 Facebook.com/HarlequinBooks

Twitter.com/HarlequinBooks

Instagram.com/HarlequinBooks

Pinterest.com/HarlequinBooks

ReaderService.com

EXPLORE.

Sign up for the Harlequin e-newsletter and
download a free book from any series at
TryHarlequin.com

CONNECT.

Join our Harlequin community to
share your thoughts and connect
with other romance readers!
Facebook.com/groups/HarlequinConnection

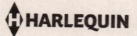

HSOCIAL2020